The Great Esc~Ape

Book 1

I0575776

BY

SEAN PATRICK JOYCE

Copyright © 2025 Sean Patrick Joyce

All rights reserved.

No part of this publication may be reproduced, stored in a retrieval system, or transmitted in any form or by any means—electronic, mechanical, photocopying, recording, or otherwise—without the prior written permission of the author, except in the case of brief quotations used in reviews or scholarly works.

ISBN: 979-8-9994844-1-3

To my parents and family, and to my teacher, Ms Nancy.

Table of Contents

Prologue: vi

Chapter 1 Outsiders Are Unwelcome 1

Chapter 2 Grandpa's Tale 15

Chapter 3 The Snake..23

Chapter 4 The Trap..29

Chapter 5 The Council's Decision 41

Chapter 6 The Monkey And The Snake 49

Chapter 7 Plans And Parrots......................................61

Chapter 8 Human Food Stinks 65

Chapter 9 Doctor Nile...71

Chapter 10 Second Thoughts.....................................75

Chapter 11 A Rift In The Plan 85

Chapter 12 Percy The Parrot......................................95

Chapter 13 The Maze Of Death................................105

Chapter 14 Peter's Story...111

Chapter 15 Apes Can't Swim....................................121

Chapter 16 Persistent Humans 131

Chapter 17 Lucky Bongo 135

Chapter 18 Percy's Secret Mission 145

Chapter 19 Broken Humans 151

Chapter 20 Plush's Secret...159

Chapter 21 Percy's Warning..167

Chapter 22 The Crazy Cursed Collar 173

Chapter 23 The Trap 185

Chapter 24 An Easy Kill 197

Chapter 25 The War Begins 207

Chapter 26 Almost Home..213

Chapter 27 The Monkey Massacre 219

Chapter 28 The Only Witness....................................229

Epilogue..237

Meet The Author 240

Prologue:

The village of Ng'ombe Miji was an isolated community in a remote area of Kenya. Ng'ombe Miji means "cow city" in Swahili, the language of Kenya. The village was a quiet place, far from any other town. In fact, it was over fifty miles to get to other human beings. As reflected by the name of their village, the villagers were cattle farmers. They lived simple lives far from the hustle and bustle and pandemonium of our society, as they say. In Ng'ombe Miji, there were more cows than people. The village was small, counting only seven buildings; there were only two rows of houses and a larger building at one end. A reasonable distance out of the village, a pasture the size of a football field was filled with -- you guessed it -- cows. Over a hundred large, hairy cows.

The villagers had lived in these parts so long, their village could quite possibly be one of the oldest human settlements on earth. Their way of life had not changed much since their village was founded; they didn't own cars or cell phones or anything resembling twenty-first century life.

Each night, a few of the villagers stayed awake to tend the fires. They did this to keep animals like lions, hyenas, and mosquitoes away from their homes. Our story begins on a dark November night when the moon was full but hiding behind the clouds, and two villagers were tending to the fires.

"I told Akida we have to set guards in the fields, or soon there won't be a single cow left," Chakka, the tall thin man, said in anger.

"We can't. We would violate our village's most ancient law -- never leave the village at night. We would anger the spirits!" roared Vanam, the oldest man in the group.

They were, of course, referring to the recent predicament that had been plaguing their village. Every night for the past two weeks, the villagers would wake to find that one cow had vanished from the pasture. There were no bodies, and the fence was too tall for a lion or leopard to jump over; and there was also no sign of any animal digging a tunnel. The village council was discussing what to do, but so far, they had not come to a decision.

Chakka and Vanam were not on the council. They were just two of the villagers who were sitting around a campfire, drinking. They had been drinking for the last few hours and were now drunk. Thus, they considered doing things they would never have done had they been sober.

"We should go wait in bushes outside the pasture. We'll be back before dawn," said Chakka.

The other man took another sip of beer. "Fine," said Vanam who stood up, wobbling a little, and barked at a passing man.

"Hey, Nash, go grab some guns. We're going to guard the pasture."

Nash was younger than the other two, still in his late teens. Eagerly, he jumped up and ran into one of the houses. A few seconds later, he returned with a rusty rifle, a sawed-off shotgun, and a flashlight. Together, the three men tiptoed out of the village and set off for the cow pasture, unaware of the danger lurking in the field.

There were two gates on either side of the rectangular plot of land: one facing the village and the other facing the silent savannah. About a mile and a half away, the men could see the faint outline of a large forest, its tall, dark trees swaying in the wind. And beyond the forest, they could faintly hear the sound of waves crashing against the beach. Unfortunately, the flashlight was not working, but none of them wanted to go back to the village and risk missing the next abduction.

The three men hid in a bush outside the gate facing the village and waited... for what? They did not know. Hours passed. They had no way to tell the time, but around 4 am, when the effects of the alcohol had started to wear off, Chakka said, "It's no use. Whatever is taking the cows took a night off."

Reluctantly, they decided to go back to the village. Vanman and Chakka stood up, but Nash didn't move.

"Come on, Nash, we don't want to get caught outside after curfew," said Vanman.

But Nash remained seated.

"Come on, Nash, do you really think whatever is taking the cows will come now? It's almost dawn," said Chakka. But Nash still didn't move; he stood still as a statue staring across the field.

"Oh, come, Nash, do you think whatever is taking the cows will appear out of nowhere? This is pointless..." Vanman stopped mid-sentence and stared in the direction Nash was looking.

The full moon gleamed down on the gate opposite where they were hiding, and a terrifying sight met their eyes: a long, black, hairy arm with fingers much too long for a person was rising slowly out of the tall grass just outside the far gate. Chakka and Vanman tried to see the rest of the creature, but the grass was too tall and dense. Slowly, the arm reached for the latch holding the gate and flicked it open. The gate creaked and slid open. The men hiding behind the bush looked at each other with fear, but it was curiosity, not daring, that held them rooted to the spot. They were not as scared as you would think. After all, they had guns, and they were all exceptionally good with firearms. They waited. They could see nothing of the mysterious creature, but they saw the gate close with a creak. Immediately, the cows erupted into panic, mooing loudly and running around the pasture, bumping into each other. The three men could not see what was causing the chaos, but they could make out what looked like black, hairy bumps moving through the field.

After about five minutes--though it felt like a lot longer to Chakka, Vanman, and Nash--one of the cows, an older cow, moved to the edge of the fence, breathing loudly, panting and gasping for air. The cow moved up to the wall only a few feet away from them.

Suddenly, something very big and very hairy came flying up from the grass right next to them, leaping through the air. It was holding what looked like an eight-foot-long spear, and with a deafening roar, the creature did a backflip in the air and landed on top of the old cow. It happened so quickly that the three men had only a second to see it. Then Chakka's rifle went off with a BANG, and the creature and cow fell and disappeared into the tall grass.

Vanam, Nash, and Chakka did not wait to see what had become of the cow. They tore back up the road toward the village, screaming about monsters and demons. They ran into the village square shouting hysterically, and Chakka grabbed a large bell and began banging it with his rifle. GONG! GONG! GONG! The noise echoed around the village (though in truth the alarm bell was not even that necessary in this situation as the gunshot had been more than enough to wake the town) Lights flicked on in all the huts, and people came tearing out into the square. This particular bell was only rung during emergencies. The last time they rang it, a pride of lions had wandered into the village boundaries; the time before that, the pasture gate had been left open, and almost all the cows had wandered off. Though the emergencies were different every time, it always meant the same thing: something was very wrong.

Five minutes later, sixteen villagers armed to the teeth came flooding down the path toward the cow field. The pasture was empty. No cow bodies, no creepy creatures. Now that dawn had started to show itself, it was a lot less eerie. And when the cows were counted, there was one less than the previous day. But when the villagers heard Chakka, Vanam, and Nash's story, they, of course, thought that the three men had been drunk and imagined it all. Vanam, Chakka, and

Nash were reprimanded for leaving the village at night by the chief, Akida.

As the villagers headed back to the town, Nash, Chakka, and Vanam stood staring out into the savannah. They saw nothing.

About a mile away, moving quickly and quietly, nine large, hairy creatures dragged a cow's body through the tall, dense grass toward the distant forest. They stopped after a few miles to catch their breath. Then they burst into laughter, screeching and howling, revealing rotten, misshapen teeth and bright eyes filled with dark pleasure.

Back in the village, Nash, Vanam, and Chakka were in one of the huts having a muttered conversation--well, at least Vanam and Nash were. Chakka stood silently, and it wasn't until Nash said his name several times that he looked up.

"Chakka, WHAT THE HELL WAS THAT THING?" said Nash, shaking with fear. Chakka didn't answer; he sat down and stared out the small window, thinking.

"Could it have been a person in a costume?" said Nash.

"No, you saw the way it jumped. An Olympic gymnast couldn't jump that high, much less carry a spear that size with them. No, whatever that thing was, it was no human," said Vanam.

Finally, Chakka joined in. He stared at them with a strange look in his eyes as if he was in a trance.

"You know when that thing jumped and landed on the cow, and I shot at it?"

"Yeah," said Nash.

Chakka paused for a second, and then, whispering so quietly that the other men could barely hear him, he muttered, "I think I hit it..."

CHAPTER 1
Outsiders are Unwelcome

The nine apes finally reached the forest. Dragging the large cow was exhausting. Panting, they were relieved of their burden by the arrival of a second group of apes. One of the apes from the new arrivals stepped forward. This ape's name was Mucha. He was the son of the chimps' chief, Travis. Mucha was a large hairy ape with a dark sneering face.

"You're late," he said in the language of the apes (which to a human would have been nothing but a mix of squeals, grunts, and violet hand gestures.)

The leader of the first group, a taller, thinner ape with a more athletic build stepped forward. This ape was named Brandon; he bowed shamefully.

"Sorry, Mucha, we were delayed in arriving because Jayden has been wounded," he said.

"How so?" asked Mucha.

"He got shot by humans," said Brandon.

"What?" roared Mucha.

"It was all Plush's fault. It was his idea not to scout the area before we took the cow," said Brandon angrily.

Brandon pointed at a smaller ape near the back of the group; this one--Plush--was different then the others. He was small, much smaller than any of the others. He also looked quite odd. His body was tall and skinny, and he had a white patch of hair on the tip of his head that stuck out quite miserably. (It was well-known that in the ape language, the word Plush means small and unimportant.)

The ape, Jayden, a younger muscular ape, shorter than Brandon, but stouter and more muscular, came forward, being half-dragged by another chimpanzee; his fingers were clamped on his left thigh where blood was pouring. He stopped in front of Mucha. Mucha turned and barked at one of the apes behind him.

"Take Jayden to the infirmary!" He turned back to the hunters.

"The rest of you come. The ape council will need to debrief you."

****

(Now, dear reader, I must make the smallest of interruptions. Do not fret, we will be back to the story soon.)

If you have never seen a chimpanzee before or are unfamiliar with the species, let us change that.

Chimpanzees are small apes, part of the animal group GREAT APES, which includes gorillas, orangutans, and humans; yes, humans. Chimpanzees are naturally found only in parts of middle and southern Africa. Chimpanzees usually walk on all fours, but sometimes they walk upright like humans. When doing this, chimps stand around 3-5 ft tall. Adult chimps weigh about 70-130 pounds. Chimpanzees might resemble short-hunched humans at times; however, chimps' arms are much longer in comparison to their bodies than human arms, and their legs are much shorter than human legs. They generally live in forests, and their diet is a mix of plants and animals. Chimps' entire bodies are covered in thick black fur. Their faces, the palms of their hands, and the bottoms of their feet are hairless.

Now back to the story.

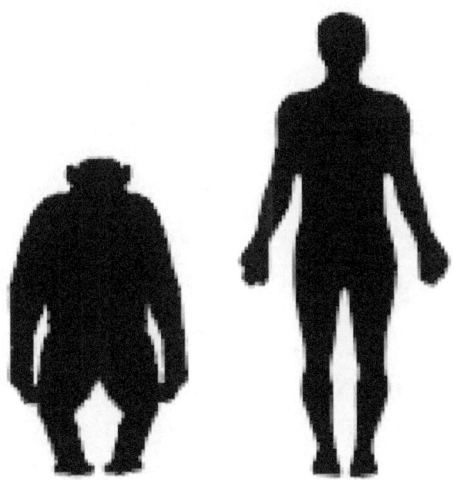

****

The group of apes turned and, walking on all fours, headed into the forest. Five minutes later, the remaining eight hunters were standing in front of the ape council--a collection of ugly, old chimpanzees. The leader, Travis, was the biggest ape in the tribe-- well over 200 pounds--and quite possibly the ugliest ape in the world. His face was covered in scorch marks from the time he had been attacked by a human with a blow torch. Travis stood at 5 foot 5 (which is very tall for a chimpanzee). His chest was more muscular than any of the other apes. He was a few years older than any of the young hunters and far more aggressive. Travis had a nasty temper, as you will soon see.

"So let me get this straight," said Travis, his deep monstrous voice echoing through the forest. "You did not follow the plan, and you purposely made yourself known to the humans? JUST HOW DUMB ARE YOU ALL??"

The hunters bowed shamefully, but one of them, towards the back of the group, stepped forward in anger.

"You're one to talk. I didn't see you risking your neck to get food for the tribe."

All the hunters gasped. The speaker was Plush. The small, runty ape was standing to the left of the group of chimpanzees.

A look of shock momentarily appeared on Travis' face, who was shocked that an ape so small would dare insult him, but this face of surprise was instantly replaced by a horrible hideous RAGE.

"HOW DARE YOU TALK TO ME LIKE THAT, YOU INSIGNIFICANT RUNT!" bellowed Travis. "IT IS YOUR FAULT THAT JAYDEN GOT HURT AND THAT THE HUMANS NOW KNOW WHO IS TAKING THEIR COWS. I DON'T KNOW HOW YOU EVEN BECAME A HUNTER! YOU AREN'T EVEN FROM THIS SAVANNAH. YOU ARE AN OUTSIDER, AND OUTSIDERS ARE UNWELCOME!"

Now Plush was filled with rage; how dare this old coward talk to him like that! He had no idea how hard it was to cross a deadly savannah at night and then sneak into a cow field and try to hunt a 2000-pound cow in an area so dense you could barely see a few feet in front of you. Had he been smarter, Plush would have kept his mouth shut, but he was a bit of what humans call a hothead. He hesitated for a moment then spoke up.

"My grandfather saved your monkey butt from a python when you were a baby. He is an outsider just like me."

Travis's face turned blood red. Calling an ape a "monkey" was extremely insulting in the ape culture. Travis was furious that the little ape talking back to him had compared him to a dumb, stupid creature like a monkey. In a fit of rage, he lunged at the young ape and shoved him to the ground before roaring into his face, "YOUR GRANDFATHER EARNED HIS PLACE IN THIS TRIBE. YOU DID NOT. THE DAY HE DIES--AND AT HIS AGE, THAT DAY IS LIKELY TO COME SOON--I WILL ENSURE THAT YOU ARE EXPELLED FROM THIS TRIBE!!"

Tears filled Plush's eyes. He tried to fight them, but they bled down his cheeks anyway. This forest was his home; he had lived here pretty much all his life; he was just a kid! Plush also knew that without the tribe, he would be completely lost. Apes needed to stay together to survive.

"You can't do that!" he cried.

"I can do whatever I want," said Travis. "I AM THE CHIEF, AND YOU ARE JUST AN UGLY, STUPID, PATHETIC LITTLE RUNT..."

Plush felt his body burn with primal anger--the kind of anger so strong it can only lead to one thing: violence. With a roar of rage, the tiny ape kicked Travis in the groin. Plush jumped up, and Travis screamed in agony and charged after him. Plush ran into a clearing in the very heart of the forest. They faced each other, each on one side of the clearing. Apes gathered around the edges, cheering and hooting, and the fight began. Plush was a decent fighter, stronger than most chimps his size, but it was the horrid burnt beast in front of him who would come out victorious. Travis punched Plush, Travis kicked Plush, and Travis karate-chopped Plush. Plush struck Travis in the rib cage. It was over in a minute. Plush was thrown to the ground, and Travis stood over him.

"I hope this taught you some manners, boy," he growled. He stood up, turned, and began to walk away. Plush, filled with rage, adrenaline, and pride, seized a stone lying on the ground and threw it very hard at the massive chimpanzee. It hit Travis hard in the back of his head, causing a massive bruise to form. Travis turned and roared so loudly that Vanam, Chakka, and Nash, almost five miles away, heard the noise.

"YOU DARE STRIKE ME WHEN MY BACK IS TURNED, COWARD?"

Travis practically flew toward Plush, ignoring the fact that attacking an opponent half your size is rarely a courageous feat.

Before Plush knew what had happened, Travis was on top of him, punching him repeatedly. Plush felt his body break. Travis punched and Travis punched. One of Plush's sharp teeth broke. Travis raised his bloodstained fist, about to strike Plush again when suddenly, a loud commanding voice bellowed "STOP."

Travis looked around, and when he realized who the speaker was, he slowly and angrily lowered his fists and reluctantly backed away from Plush.

The speaker was a very old ape who was slowly making his way into the clearing. Chimps age quicker than humans so this ape, who was roughly fifty-six in human years, was closer to seventy-five in ape years. Like Plush, this ape was different then any of the other chimps in the clearing. Most noticeably was the fact that this ape was walking upright on two legs instead of four; he also carried a large wooden stick with him which he used as a cane to balance himself. His fur was covered in old battle wounds and his face was lined with faded scars. He was a small ape about the same size as Plush, though he had been larger when he was younger.

The apes surrounding the clearing fell silent, all eyes now pointing at the newcomer. The old ape came walking properly into the clearing, stopping in front of Travis and Plush. He looked around until his ancient eyes fell on Plush who was still laying on the ground.

"You, boy, get up now," he said, his voice sharp and commanding. Plush rose slowly to his feet as he stood facing the old ape. He opened his mouth and tried to say, "Grandpa, it's…"

"SILENCE!" shouted the old ape, and raising his cane, he struck young Plush across the face.

Plush stumbled back looking both angry and annoyed.

The old ape turned facing Travis, his old eyes filled with anger.

"Travis, what is the meaning of this? I awake not to the sounds of cheering and the joy of a successful hunt, but to the chaos of shouts and screeches. When I come to investigate, what do I find? YOU, the leader of the tribe, attacking my grandson with deadly intent. Explain yourself NOW!"

Travis glared at the old ape with hatred and anger. .

"Elder Purcellville, your grandson insulted me. He called me a coward, a fool, a MONKEY. He said I have done nothing to help the tribe. I refuse to allow anyone to speak to me that way. ANYONE!"

The old ape, Purcellville, sighed deeply

"Travis, you are many things, but a coward is certainly not one of them. LOOK!" and the old ape pointed his cane at multiple points on Travis' body. "The scars you bear on your body are proof of your courageous actions. Look at the burn marks on your face. Remember how you saved this tribe from that crazy fire-wielding human? Not one of the many apes here was able to stop the human, but you did, Travis. You are the first and only chimpanzee in this tribe to not only survive a fight with a human but win one, and you were just a child at the time! And, not only that, there are the claw marks on your back-- you got those when you single-handedly killed that leopard who had a large appetite for ape flesh. And then, there are the marks on your shoulder from when you saved MY life from those two mandrills last winter on our scouting expedition. Nearly every ape in this tribe owes you a great debt."

Travis smiled proudly. Clearly, he enjoyed being reminded of his many victories.

But Purrcellvile was not done talking.

"But, Travis, do not forget that it was I who saved **you** from a python years ago when you were just an infant. I defeated that snake singlehandedly with this very branch. " He gestured to his cane and continued. "Travis, I apologize for my grandson's foolish actions, but don't let the careless words of a foolish and immature child affect you.. Because that is what my grandson is: A CHILD. After everything this tribe has been through, I would hope we could move beyond these absurd gladiator fights."

Purcellville finished speaking and there was silence from everyone; even the birds in the surrounding trees had stopped their squawking to listen. Purcellville was a quiet, old ape. He had never been the biggest or strongest. In fact, even in his younger years he had been relatively small for a male chimpanzee. But Purcellville's real strength was not his fists; it was his mind. Unlike the thuggish, simple-minded chimps that surrounded him, Purcellville had a very human way of thinking. He was able to control his temper; he always spoke formally; and his dialect was much more advanced than any other non-human creature. He was well-respected by all the apes, even Travis. For this reason, all the surrounding animals were silent, waiting for the old ape to continue talking.

Purcellville, however, did not continue the conversation. He stopped talking and started sniffing the air and glancing nervously around the clearing.

Plush could feel it too; an eerie chill seemed to surround them.

Suddenly, Brandon, the headhunter chimpanzee, came charging into the clearing, shouting.

"THE BABOONS! THE BABOONS ARE ATTACKING!"

Panic flew through the chimpanzee tribe. The baboons were large monkeys that lived in groups up north of the ape forest, outnumbering the chimpanzees by about five to one. Travis jumped up and began to run among the apes shouting things like, "BATTLE STATIONS!" and "PREPARE TO KILL!"

Then, there were baboons. Lots of baboons. Large baboons, ugly baboons. The baboons lived across the river a few miles to the north of the ape forest and, unlike the chimpanzees, did not need to live in forests to survive. The baboons were not struggling like the apes; all the herds had migrated up north across the river and right into baboon territory. The apes couldn't swim, and so the river prevented them from ever going upstream; baboons could swim, and, as a result, they had plenty of food. But the baboons still enjoyed raiding the apes. There were about fifty baboons attacking (although there were many more in their tribe). They had swum across the river in the early hours of the morning, and their tan-colored fur made it easy to camouflage in the dry savannah grass. These baboons were of a species known to humans as chacma baboons. Chacma baboons have grayish-tan colored fur and long tails. Their fur covers their entire bodies except for their faces which are similar to chimpanzees' faces. It's their mouths that are different. While chimps have two small, pointed fangs, chacmas have long jutted jaws and dagger-like fangs double the size of the chimps'.. Full grown baboons are roughly equal in size to chimpanzees though not as intelligent.

Though attacking baboons rarely killed the chimpanzees in Travis' pack; however, they enjoyed causing massive injuries to the chimps and often stole what little food the apes could round up. The old ape, Purcellville, pushed his grandson to the ground and rushed forward into the battle. A baboon rushed at him but, with surprising speed and agility, the old ape beat the monkey relentlessly with his cane until the monkey gave up and scampered off.

Plush felt weak and scared. He fled up a tree and hid in the dense leaves. He watched as chaos broke out among the apes. The world was fists and claws as apes and baboons rolled around fighting. Plush could see Travis, Brandon, and Mucha all fighting fiercely; all of his fellow hunters were also fighting monkeys. As Plush scanned the battlefield, he could see Jayden, the hunter ape who Chakka had shot, lying on the ground being attacked by a particularly large baboon. Jayden was too wounded to fight back and was close to death. No one else seemed to notice. The rest of the apes were too busy fighting and too distracted to do anything. Plush knew he had to help, but he was already hurt, and he knew he was no match for the large monkey.

Before Plush could decide what to do, the branch he was standing on broke, and he fell, screaming through the air. He managed to grab onto a vine and swing into the air, but his momentum was too great and he crashed into another tree. The impact of the crash caused him to lose his grip on the vine, and he fell right into a large, spiky thorn bush. Hearing the noise, the apes and baboons stopped fighting to watch, but as soon as Plush fell into the bush and let out a high-pitched scream, they looked back at each other, shrugged, and went back to fighting. Plush emerged from the thornbush covered in thorns, yowling like a demented cat.

Shaking the thorns off him, he realized that he was standing in the middle of a war; apes and monkeys were rolling around, fighting all around him. Through the chaos, he spotted Jayden still being beaten to a pulp by the baboon. Plush did not really remember what happened next. He seemed to move as if in a trance, and before he knew what had happened, he was standing over the baboon who was attacking Jayden. The aggressive monkey was so busy beating up the wounded chimpanzee he did not realize Plush was right behind him. Up close, Plush realized just how big the baboon was: he was nearly twice Plush's size. (And, though Plush did not know it at the time, this monkey happened to be the baboon king, Bruno.)

Then Plush did something very brave and very stupid. He jumped forward, grabbed the baboon around the neck, and sank his teeth into Bruno's shoulder. Bruno screamed and reared up, standing on two legs. Madly, he ran around the clearing with Plush piggyback-riding him. Finally, Bruno's hands found Plush's face. The next thing Plush knew, for the second time in less than an hour, he was lying on his back being beaten by an enraged primate--but this time, it was the baboon king.

Bruno was punching his victim the same way Travis had. Plush was squealing like a pig as his hands desperately groped around on the ground until he found what he was looking for--a stone. Bruno was just about to end Plush's life with his razor-sharp fangs when Jayden--covered in blood and limping--punched Bruno from behind. It was a feeble blow, given Jayden's physical state, but it distracted Bruno long enough. WHAM! The stone in Plush's hands banged against Bruno's skull. Bruno jumped back, screaming in pain, but he recovered quickly and turned to face Plush again--Plush raised his fist and was about to hurl it at Bruno, but with an evil grin, the massive monkey simply stepped aside and allowed Plush to sail past him. The force of his swing propelled Plush into a tree. He turned, shaking his dizzy head, and charged at Bruno once more, but despite his huge size, the monkey king easily dodged him, and Plush flew past him again. He tried attacking Bruno from the side, but Bruno was bigger, stronger, and faster--much faster. He seemed to be toying with Plush by allowing the young chimp to attack him but not actually hurt him. This game of "dodge the danger" went on for quite some time until...POW!

Finally, Plush struck true, and his bloodstained fist went sailing across Bruno's face. Bruno staggered back and Plush thought he had an opening; he scrambled up the closest tree trunk and jumped. Kicking outward with his legs, he flew towards Bruno, but unfortunately for Plush, Bruno was not as injured as he looked, and with one hand, he grabbed Plush out of the air, flipped the ape over, and sent him flying towards a tree head first. Plush felt the tree connect with his skull, and he remembered no more...

CHAPTER 2
Grandpa's Tale

When Plush came to, he opened his eyes to see apes running around in a panic. There was no sign of the baboons. Plush sighed with relief, but it was short-lived.

"THEY TOOK THE COW! THEY TOOK THE COW!"

It was Brandon. In all the chaos, no one had seen a group of baboons drag away the corpse of the cow the chimpanzees so desperately needed.

"After them! We have to stop them before they reach the river!" said Mucha.

A large group of chimpanzees took off running after the fleeing baboons. Plush was about to join them, but he felt a hand on his shoulder, turned around, and saw his grandfather, Purcellville standing over him. The elderly ape slowly shook his head, motioning for Plush to follow him back to their hut in the trees. Plush grudgingly followed. The two apes climbed up a large tree with many twists and turns until they reached an area of the trunk where there was a large hollowed-out room; it would not seem very big to you or me, but to an ape, it was a mansion.

A few minutes later Plush was standing in the center room watching his grandfather pace back and forth in front of him, berating him for his actions. Though he was obviously furious, the old ape spoke in his characteristic measured tones.

"I can not believe you talked back to a head councilman, much less Travis," said his grandfather. "You could have died! If you upset Travis again like that I won't be able to stop him. I can see it in his eyes. My strength is fading. It's only a matter of time before he is outside of my control and reasoning. Plush, do you think after what you did today he will even consider allowing you to become a member of the tribe? I know Travis can be cold and cruel at times but have some sense. What did you think would come out of picking a fight with the biggest, strongest ape in the tribe? And not only that, Brandon told me that you convinced your fellow hunters not to scout the pasture before hunting. You all could have been killed!"

"It was not my fault," said Plush. "Jayden was the one who spooked the humans, not me."

"SILENCE!" his grandfather roared, and he once again whacked Plush across the face with his cane.

"Why can't you ever take responsibility for your actions? If you had scouted the area like you were supposed to, you would have seen the humans! We won't be able to take any more cows after tonight. Don't you understand? You made us lose the only source for food we have! The whole tribe is going to go hungry for who knows how long, and, not only will we starve, but if you had done what you were told to do, Jayden wouldn't be dying in the infirmary right now! All of this...BECAUSE OF YOU!"

"How could I have known the humans would be hiding in the bushes? We've never seen one outside the village at night before," said Plush. "I WAS JUST TRYING TO HELP!"

His grandfather sighed. "I know you are trying to get noticed and accepted into the tribe, but you can't put apes in unnecessary danger. You don't choose your moment to get accepted, Plush. That moment chooses you."

"Easy for you to say; you got accepted by sheer luck when a random snake tried to eat all the baby apes," grumbled Plush.

They continued their argument for another twenty minutes, and after delivering several more whacks from his cane, Purcellville sighed, sat down, and glared at Plush.

"I promised your parents I would protect you; it was their dying wish for me to keep you safe."

"Well, I don't need you to protect me! I can take care of myself," said Plush.

"Well, when you come of age in a few months, you can make your own decisions, but while you're still a child, you will do what I tell you. DO YOU UNDERSTAND, Plush?" he bellowed angrily.

Plush groaned, turned around, and was about to leave when he heard sniffling behind him. He turned and saw his grandfather sitting on the floor of the cave, sobbing softly.

"I still think about her every day: your mother, my daughter."

Tears fell from his grandfather's face and Plush moaned silently, annoyed. He knew what his grandfather was about to do; he was going to tell Plush the story of his parents' death. Plush had heard it so many times he knew it back to front.

Thirteen years before (thirteen in human years, seventeen in ape years), Plush, his parents, his grandparents, and about fifteen other apes had been living in another forest a few dozen miles from this one. According to his grandfather, Plush, who was only a few weeks old at the time, had been taking a nap when the attack happened. Plush did not know exactly how it had played out. But the story always started the same way, with a BANG--a real bang, a noise so loud that the trees shook, the birds took flight, and apes screamed and ran around in a panic shouting for their loved ones. The noise had awoken Plush, and he screamed in wide-eyed terror. Being a young ape, he had never heard a noise like that before, but his grandfather, Purcellville, knew only one thing that could make a sound like that: a gun, a human gun. The noise had thrown baby Plush into a frenzy. He ran around the little nest his mother had made for him in the low-hanging branches of a large tree. According to his grandfather, the old ape had grabbed Plush out of the nest and dove into a thick bush, completely concealing them from sight. A minute later, Plush's parents followed after them, completely hidden from sight. The four apes huddled together, not daring to move.

All around them, they could hear the thunderous bangs that were the guns of humans and the agonizing screams of dying apes. Minutes passed, though it felt like days to the apes. Finally, the noise died down--literally, in some cases. And then it was gone. No more screaming apes. No more gunfire, just silence. No birds. No insects. No wind. It was as if all the earth was holding its breath. Although it was quiet now, the four apes stayed huddled in the bushes. Just when they thought it was safe to come out, they heard the sound of approaching footsteps, and through a small hole near the bottom of the bush, they saw them: two pairs of boots that stopped a few inches from where they were hiding and two tall smelly humans, both male by the looks of them. They were having a heated conversation. The apes could see that the humans were caucasian, and they both had large rifles in their hands.

They were speaking in the odd sizzling grunts that must have been the language of the humans, and though the apes heard them, they did not understand the language. The first human was a large young fat man with short blonde hair who was shorter than his companion but at least twice as wide. The second man looked to be a few years older than the first man and from the way he was speaking, he seemed to be the leader. If the apes had been able to understand them then they would have heard the first man say, "MAN, that was the craziest thing I've ever done. It reminds me of the time we got lost on Mount Rushmore back in '98…WOAH!"

The second man swung around and shoved his companion aggressively, knocking him off balance. The younger man shouted angrily. "WHAT THE HELL WAS THAT FOR, THOMAS?"

The second human ignored his companions' outburst and responded with an angry monologue. "YOU YOU FOOL! YOU MYPOIC, MINDLESS, CHILD! DO YOU KNOW WHAT YOUR ACTIONS HAVE COST ME? I CAME HERE TO CAPTURE THESE CREATURES ALIVE--TO STUDY THEM--BUT WHAT DO? YOU PANIC AT THE FIRST SIGN OF MOVEMENT AND SHOOT ONE OF THE APES YOU MADE THE REST OF THEM TO ATTACK US. THEN, WITHOUT SO MUCH AS A THOUGHT IN THAT MINISCULE BRAIN OF YOURS, YOU AND YOUR DELINQUENT FRIENDS START SHOOTING ALL OF THEM! WHAT WAS GOING TO BE MY MOST VALUABLE SPECIMEN, MAY BE LOST BECAUSE OF YOU! YEARS OF RESEARCH AND SEARCHING MAY ALL BE FOR NOTHING…" And then, more quietly, in a sinister voice he said, "tell me, Benjamin, are all the apes dead?"

"I…I think so, Mr. Winson," said Ben, slowly getting to his feet. "Nile flew the drone over the forest a few days ago, and we counted about eighteen apes."

"And how many have been killed?" asked Mr. Winson, his voice dangerously quiet. Ben hesitated before giving the news.

"Sixteen dead--the one Yori shot in the stomach with an arrow is still breathing, but it's losing blood quickly."

"WELL THEN, GO CLEAN THE CUT, STITCH THE WOUND, AND KEEP IT ALIVE, OR I SWEAR, BENJAMIN, YOU WILL WISH YOU WERE DEAD!"

Ben nodded, turned, and hurriedly scampered away muttering angrily,"You would have shot it, too, if it had landed right on THE TOP OF YOUR HEAD!"

Meanwhile, the four apes prayed that the other, more terrifying human would follow. If he didn't leave soon, they might have to attack him to escape, and as long as he had his rifle, trying to escape was a death sentence. They couldn't stay there forever. Unfortunately, he showed no sign of departing. He sat on the ground, and they saw his face: he was Caucasian with dark brown hair. He looked to be in his early-30s, but it was his eyes that alarmed them. The man's left eye was dark brown, but his right eye was deep blue. The apes didn't understand genetics and assumed these humans were monsters (and considering what they had done to the forest, the apes were not totally wrong in their thinking).

The man pulled a ham and cheese sandwich out of his pocket and began to eat, his rifle in his lap. The smell of ham and cheese was agonizing to the apes, and watching this human munch on food without a care in the world while they had to risk their lives daily just to get something to eat was quite unbearable. Finally, the human finished his sandwich and stood up.

"Please go, please go, please go," the apes silently prayed.

The man, Mr. Winson, then pulled out a whistle and blew a sharp high note. Immediately, the apes heard footsteps--but not human footsteps. Through the trees, an enormous dog the size of a bear came bounding out of the woods and into the clearing. The dog was a large brown English mastiff, a natural hunter. It was at that moment the apes knew they were dead. That dog would smell them even if they were miles away.

The man patted the dog on the head, and then he bent down and muttered something. It was as if he was speaking to the vicious creature.

Even in all the suspense, years later, his grandfather would always tell Plush how strange it was that the dog, which was close to a lion in size and could crush the human with a single bite from his jaws, would ever take orders from something so much smaller and weaker than itself. But the dog not only communicated with the human but seemed to take orders from it as though the human was the master and the dog was a servant. (Of course, as we know, the human *was* its master, but apes are only apes, after all.)

The dog began to sniff the air. Then, it looked directly at the bush and gave a single loud bark. The human turned slowly and bent over the bush. They heard his rifle click. He was about to part the greenery that protected them when suddenly a loud rustling noise came from behind him. He whirled around just in time to see a lone ape come hurtling out of the dense brush from the other side of the clearing. The ape, who was running full speed on four legs, didn't seem to register the danger of its surroundings. Startled, it saw the human, and then, as the two most common danger senses--fight and flight-- kicked in, this ape decided on both. It flew at the human with incredible speed.

The dog lunged toward it, but the ape jumped in the air, flipped over the dog, and landed on the human causing them both to topple over. Mr. Winson, the human, seemed so shocked at the ape doing something so stupid he didn't even react until the ape ran around him and went tearing away in the brush.

The dog charged after it, barking and yapping. The human jumped up and muttered, "Let's see how fast you are when I blow your leg off!" He stood and raised his rifle at the retreating ape. The apes in the bush heard the spring snap.

Seeing their opening, Plush's parents dove out of their hiding space and rushed at the distracted human. Plush's grandfather did not know exactly what happened next; he grabbed baby Plush and made a mad dash out of the forest, where he knew he could take refuge in the tall grass of the savannah. The last thing his grandfather saw was Plush's mother pounding her fist into the human's face, and Plush's father biting at the human's fingers. He didn't see that the human's other hand was free--and desperately reaching for his rifle. Then they heard two loud bangs, then quiet, and then a final bang. Silence. Clutching Plush, his grandfather turned away from the forest, tears falling down his face as he quietly bounded away into the tall grass.

Mr. Winson was lying unconscious next to the two ape corpses when Ben returned. At first, he thought his boss had succumbed to his injuries, but the human was stirring. Mr. Winson opened his mismatched eyes, looking around at the forest. He tried to speak, but his damaged jaw didn't seem to be working. He stood up glaring daggers at Ben, and then he gazed at the sea of savannah grass. Without a sound, he turned back to face Ben and the two men walked away.

CHAPTER 3
The Snake

Plush stormed out of their nest and began climbing back down the tree, away from his grandfather.

"Hey! I wasn't finished with the story! Get back here," shouted Purcellville.

Plush ignored him and walked away into the clearing. All around him, apes were busy treating the wounded, organizing weapons, and digging for termites. Plush walked to the edge of the forest and climbed a young tree at the edge of the forest overlooking the savannah; he sat down on a high branch and groaned. He knew he shouldn't have left his grandfather like that, but he had heard that same story so often that the mere mention of it angered him. He knew what happened after his grandfather escaped the humans. The two of them had traveled away from the forest into the open savannah where they met up with another ape who turned out to be the same ape who had been chased off by the dog, an alchemist named Albert Apenstien.

(No, dear reader, that is not a joke. His real name was Albert Apenstein, and he has no relation to the famous Dr. Albert Einstein that you are familiar with. The naming of this ape is definitely NOT my poor attempt at humor, whatsoever. It is mere coincidence.)

Together, the three apes set off. Because he couldn't walk very well yet, Plush rode on his grandfather's back. The apes faced many dangers getting to the other forest, including leopards, hyenas, and baboons. It got quite difficult especially with the added burden of a baby, and the threesome traveled slowly through the savannah. They also exercised extreme caution because going faster would alert animals of their presence. After ten days, they reached the southern savannah but were met with stones, sticks, and teeth. The ape tribe living there did not trust outsiders and immediately demanded that they leave, but when they realized that Plush's grandfather had a baby with him, they agreed to let them stay for one night.

During the night, one of the local apes began vomiting and coughing up blood--symptoms of the deadly Ebola virus. This set the apes into a panic, but Albert Apenstien who was a very skilled alchemist, immediately made a concoction out of a large variety of herbs, fungi, and insects. After feeding it to the sick ape, the patient slowly began to feel better, and by dawn of the next day, his fever had broken and the intense bleeding had stopped. Amazed, the tribe begged Albert to stay and became the tribe's Healer (which is what apes call doctors). Albert agreed, and after treating large numbers of sick and injured apes, all who recovered, he was immediately welcomed into the tribe with honors.

Meanwhile, Plush's grandfather had a much tougher time. Because he was Albert's friend, the tribe had allowed him to stay one more week, but knowing he would have to leave and return to the wild, endless savannah alone--with his tiny grandson to care for--was a very depressing thought. That night, they offered to keep Plush in the "nursery" with the other infant apes. Of course, it was not really a nursery but more of a clearing in the middle of the forest where the baby apes slept. Plush's grandfather did not entirely trust the tribe, so he concealed himself in a bush outside the clearing and waited. However, after a few hours, exhaustion from the past week overtook him, and he succumbed to sleep.

Around 3 a.m. when all the forest was asleep, a python by the name of Peter snuck into the forest, hoping to gobble up at least one sleeping infant. He slithered into the clearing and stealthily approached a particularly fat young ape who turned out to be none other than a much younger Travis. The python sniffed the air with his long forked tongue, and slithered towards his slumbering prey. Peter the python was about to sink his fangs into the ape when the baby rolled over, and one of his eyes opened. The terrified toddler took one look at the enormous snake and let out a very loud scream. The terrified wailing slapped Plush's grandfather awake, and he stood up just in time to see the snake lunge at the screaming infant.

"NOO!!!!!!" with a roar, Plush's grandfather launched himself at the snake, sending his fist into its face. The snake screeched and before it knew what had happened, Plush's grandfather seized a branch lying on the ground and rammed it deep into the snake's right eye. With a HISSSS of pain, the snake turned and, with surprising speed for a creature so large, fled from the clearing, spitting and cursing at the apes.

When the rest of the adult apes came to investigate the noise, they were shocked to see Plush's grandfather standing there, branch in hand, unharmed. It was obvious from the tracks and trail of blood left in the dirt that the python had been enormous. Few apes could take on even a smaller python by themselves; the tribe usually needed at least two adult males to drive off a snake of that size. The fact that Plush's grandfather had done so single-handedly was awe-inspiring and immediately gained him entrance into the tribe.

The next few years were a golden age for the apes. Albert not only had a vast knowledge of medical science but also a knack for inventing tools. The brilliant scientist introduced the tribe to weapons like the spear and tools like hammers, shovels, and knives. Plush's grandfather also proved himself to be a natural leader; he showed the apes improved hunting tactics and developed a leadership system for the ape tribe which involved a council, a chief, and an elder. With these advances, the ape tribe had a thriving food supply and strong leadership.

The Golden Age did not last, however. Several years after Albert, Purcellville, and Plush's inclusion in the tribe, fate hit the tribe with a vengeance. The dry season had come, and for some reason, it didn't leave. The savannah had seen little to no rain all season, and because of this, almost all the grazing animals had migrated away. Most of the fruit trees also failed to produce food because they did not have enough rain. The apes were starving. And this was only the beginning of their problems.

****

Plush sat in the tree, his mind rolling over the details his grandfather shared. He, of course, did not remember any of these events because he had been too young.

He was so lost in thought that he did not notice Brandon, the lead hunter, climbing up to him. The gravity of the situation did not register with him until Brandon was a few feet beneath him in the tree.

"Plush, I just spoke with the ape council, and they agreed that due to your recklessness and just plain stupidity, you have been expelled from the hunters."

"WHAT?" screamed Plush. "How is that fair?" he said.

"Plush, you're lucky you weren't banished from the forest,"

said Brandon. "This is the minimal punishment, and, anyway, you always hated being on part of the hunters."

"Yeah, but that was my last chance to get recognized and earn my place in the tribe. You know the rules. If you are not born into the tribe, you must earn your place before you turn eighteen." (Eighteen in ape years is thirteen in human years).

Brandon sighed, shook his head, and left.

Plush sat in the tree all day thinking. Why had he lost his temper with Travis? If he had kept his cool, he might still have a chance at earning his place in the tribe. He thought about his grandfather, and for a second, he imagined his grandfather trying to convince the ape council to let him stay. He sighed feeling guilty about walking out on his grandfather; he just felt so trapped by the story, the tribe, his past. Deep down, part of him wanted to be kicked out of the tribe. He would have freedom--freedom to travel anywhere. He remembered as a child staring at the stars and thinking, *This can't be all there is. There has to be more to our existence than just scavenging and struggling all our lives."*

Plush longed to see the rest of the world. He wanted to cross the distant mountains, travel endless deserts, and discover more creatures beyond the savannah. Maybe, just maybe, he would find his purpose. All the other apes didn't seem to care for such things. They were content to survive--but only to survive, not to really live. To Plush, merely surviving was not living. He sighed again.

He was starting to feel hungry; his stomach growled, but he ignored it. He was always hungry. TThere was never enough food or water for everyone. He hated his life. He hated being an orphan. He hated being an outcast. He hated being hungry. He hated the baboons. He hated Travis. And he especially hated the small voice in the back of his mind that told him he was different. The voice that reminded him that he was a mistake, a bug in the system, a heavy weight in the balance of life. Why couldn't he be more like Brandon or his grandfather, a normal chimp? Despite living with the tribe almost all his life, he never really felt at home. Maybe he was just upset because he looked different from the other apes. Most of the apes looked almost identical to each other, with the same skin color and the same instincts. Plush, with the patch of white hair on the top of his head and his stunted size, looked completely out of place. As he sat watching the grass of the endless savannah sway in the wind, Plush wondered where all these thoughts came from, what made him different and why was he different, why couldn't he be a normal ape? What was the nagging voice in his head? Something small, something unreasonable, something... *human.*

CHAPTER 4
The Trap

The villagers of Ng'ombe Miji were going about their daily lives, tending to their cattle, painting their huts, and watering their gardens when suddenly a strange noise floated through the air. The distant sound of electric guitars, drums, and drunk rappers yelling swear words seemed to vibrate through the village. Suddenly out of nowhere, a large Land Rover came speeding through the rows of houses. Its windows were tinted. Its horn was blaring, and its engine roared like a bear. The villagers scattered as the car narrowly avoided running over Nash; it tore up the road and came screeching to a halt outside the village chief, Akida's, house. The rock music cut off as the driver and side doors opened and out stepped two men.

One of them was known to the villagers as "Big Ben," an obese Irishman with short orange hair, a large red face, and a scraggly beard that ran up the sides of his face. He appeared every couple of months and rented one of the huts. During his visits, Big Ben and several other outsiders would hunt a variety of animals, but it had been almost eight months since Ben's last visit.

The second man was the physical opposite of Big Ben. He was Japanese. Though equal in height to Big Ben, he was as skinny as a wire. Equally tiresome, the second man was known as "Little John" to the villagers.

The two men walked up the steps to the chief's house, but just as Big Ben was about to open the door, they heard multiple voices yelling at the top of their lungs.

"IT WAS A DEMON, I TELL YOU! A DEMON!" said the first panicked voice.

"YOU DRUNK FOOL! THERE ARE NO SUCH THINGS AS DEMONS!" a second voice answered.

"NASH SAW THE WHOLE THING, AND HE WAS COMPLETELY SOBER," the first voice responded.

"NASH IS A CHILD. A CHILD! AND IN THE COMPANY OF TWO DRUNK MORONS, OF COURSE, HE IS GOING TO SIDE WITH YOU!" the second man shouted, his temper rising.

"FINE! DO NOTHING! BUT DON'T BLAME ME WHEN ALL THE COWS ARE GONE," the first man roared.

The door opened and out walked Chakka and the village chief, Akida, arguing like children. Akida stopped at the sight of Big Ben and Little John.

"What do you want?" he said, clearly annoyed. He spoke these words in English, the language of the newcomers.

Big Ben stepped forward and handed Akida a stack of cash-- around a hundred thousand in shillings, the currency in Kenya.

"No questions," said Little John, who also spoke in English.

Akida sighed and pointed to one of the huts. "You can stay there, but I want you gone by the end of the week," he said.

Big Ben nodded and opened the trunk of their Land Rover. He pulled out an enormous bag, the contents of which Akida didn't dare ask. The weary chief returned to his house alone. Chakka was also walking away when he felt a hand on his shoulder. He turned and saw Little John right behind him.

"Hey, pal, what was all that screaming about? My Swahili isn't perfect, but it didn't sound like you two were arguing over a bet on the World Cup," Big Ben chuckled to himself. Chakka, seeing no reason to lie or keep the previous night's events secret, happily explained everything in English including the mysterious, hairy arm and the spear-carrying creatures.

As he spoke, Big Ben and Little John listened with expressionless faces, but when he finished sharing the tale, both of them burst out laughing; they laughed until they had tears in their eyes. Chakka sighed. He knew it--no one was going to believe him. Defeated, he began to walk away, but Big Ben stopped laughing and ran after him.

"Hey, pal, we know what's taking your cows, and it ain't no demon, my friend."

Chakka, curious, asked him to explain.

"It's quite simple, mate. You have an ape problem--more specifically, a chimp problem." Chakka raised an eyebrow, skeptically.

"Chimps don't use spears, and they definitely don't sneak into pastures in the dead of night to steal one cow. If they wanted our cows, they would just take them all. And even if they did have spears, they have never come near our village before; they live in the big forest just a few miles east of here down by the beach…"

Chakka paused and considered what Big Ben had said. It almost made sense. The arm he saw could definitely belong to an ape, and the creature that spooked him did fit the description of a chimpanzee. He knew that chimps used primitive tools, but he had never heard of them using spears before. Or stealing cows. However, it was not an impossible theory.

"Man, and here I was ranting on about demons and monsters," he chuckled to himself, then stopped. "No," he said aloud. "It's not possible. Chimpanzees wouldn't do that. Sure, they're smart, but they're not THAT smart. Everybody knows that."

Little John chuckled. "You know something? If you ask any chimpanzee expert out there, they'll tell you that there are no apes living in Kenya. No one outside of your tiny town and a few lucky hunters know about the small pocket of chimps in this area," Little John stopped talking. He looked worried. Clearly, he had revealed more than he wanted to. But Big Ben cut in quickly. "Yeah, it's a goldmine for us out here," Ben said, smiling boastfully.

"You know," said Little John, "Even just one chimpanzee sells for quite a bit. We could use your help and I'm sure your little village could benefit from…"

"I'm NOT interested," said Chakka quickly--partially out of his distaste for poaching and partially out of his fear of the previous night's events.

The two men shrugged.

"No questions, remember?" Big Ben said, "But I can guarantee you this: no ape will take your cows again. We will make sure of that."

He spoke so confidently that Chakka almost forgot his fear. Big Ben and Little John turned and began walking out towards the cow field.

"Wait!" said Chakka in a slightly panicked voice. "You can't go out there at night, it's way too dangerous for two people. Those things were practically invisible. I couldn't see them clearly until they were about a foot in front of me."

Big Ben sighed. "Amateur," he muttered. Then he turned around and walked up to Chakka until they were nose to nose. "Do I look stupid to you?" he growled.

Chakka looked Big Ben up and down from the snot dribbling from his nose to his mismatched socks to his shirt inside out. Chakka longed to say, *"Yes, you do,"* but after considering how much bigger Ben was than him, he thought the better of it and decided to shift gears.

"How do you plan on capturing those things?" Chakka said.

"That's the last question we will answer," said Big Ben smugly. "We're gonna place steel bear traps all around the far side of your cow field.

"We're gonna cover them with leaves and dirt, so when the apes come tonight, at least one of them will certainly get caught. We will also set up thermal and night vision cameras that connect directly to our phones, giving us an early warning if one is trapped, and then we'll come sweeping in with guns," said Little John. "And then..."

"BANG! BANG! BANG!" they said together and high-fived each other as they walked away, leaving Chakka speechless. He was sure it was the last time he would see those two numbskulls. Even if their plan worked, they would still be facing at least a dozen apes with spears in the dead of night. Chakka was confident Big Ben and Little John would not be alive in the morning. He shrugged. If they died, then the villagers would get to keep all their belongings, their car, and all their equipment including the large amount of cash they undoubtedly had. Chakka smiled to himself and left the two outsiders to their most certain fate.

****

Plush sighed as the sun finally set and was replaced by the moon which was unusually bright, though maybe it just seemed that way because there were no clouds. He watched silently from the trees as the hunters prepared for another raid on the humans, wishing more than ever that he could join them. He knew if he tried following them, they would just force him to come back, and if he left before them, they would still stop him from participating. He could hear the parents and family members of the hunters arguing with the ape council, furious that they thought it was a good idea to send their loved ones back to the human village right after the humans discovered who was taking their cows --- especially when the moon was full. Through all the yelling and screeching, he heard his grandfather's voice among the protesters.

"Travis, this is too dangerous. We must wait. If we let the humans think we have given up, they will let their guard down. Then we can try again. We will just have to be a little hungry for a bit. I told you we were taking their cows too consistently. They may not have noticed if we took them less frequently. Now look at what has happened."

"Oh, don't start, Purcellville. It was your grandson who was responsible for Jayden's injury; Apenstein just informed me that Jayden has entered an unnatural deep sleep due to blood loss. He might not last the night. If the baboons had not attacked and stolen our cow, we would all be enjoying fresh meat and have full bellies. It is not my fault we have so many enemies, Purcellville!" Travis finished, glaring at Plush's grandfather.

Plush almost didn't recognize the name. Purcellville was indeed his grandfather's name, but Plush knew him only as "grandfather" or "grandpa." It was odd to realize how much influence his elderly relative had in the tribal council. Plush was so lost in thought he almost missed what his grandfather said next.

"Travis, the humans are not our enemies; well, at least they *weren't* our enemies. We can't have a war with humans AND baboons. Travis, I have told you many times before: the best way to defeat an enemy is to…"

"SHUT UP!" yelled Travis, cutting Purcellville off.

"THE BEST WAY TO DEFEAT AN ENEMY? OH, I DON'T KNOW? SNEAK ATTACK? CLUB THEM TO DEATH IN THEIR SLEEP? IT IS NOT YOUR DECISION OR YOUR RESPONSIBILITY TO MAKE MY DECISIONS, PURCELLVILLE. AS THE TRIBE'S ELDER YOU ARE TO ADVISE ME, NOT CONTROL ME!"

The apes broke into screeches and squeals, arguing and fighting amongst themselves.

"ATTACK THE HUMANS! BURN THEIR VILLAGE TO THE GROUND!" roared Jayden's Father.

"STOP! STOP!" yelled Plush's grandfather. "WE MUST NOT FIGHT AMONGST OURSELVES; THE HUMANS WERE JUST FIGHTING TO DEFEND THEIR CATTLE. THEY NEED IT JUST AS MUCH AS WE DO. ATTACKING THEM ONLY ESCALATES THE SITUATION. GOING TO WAR WITH HUMANS IS A TERRIBLE IDEA. HOW MANY MORE JAYDENS DO WE NEED? AND, TRAVIS, IT'S ALSO BECAUSE OF MY GRANDSON THAT JAYDEN LIVES. IF PLUSH HAD NOT STOOD UP TO BRUNO, JAYDEN WOULD BE DEAD. WE DON'T KNOW IF JAYDEN IS GOING TO DIE. HE MAY YET PULL THROUGH!"

Albert Apenstain stepped forward and spoke. "I agree. We can't attack humans. They have weapons far superior to ours, and personally, I don't want to get caught on the wrong side of one of their guns again."

Albert shared a look with Purcellville who knew more than anyone what AGAIN meant. Angry voices rose from all directions and soon nothing was audible.

(If you or I, dear reader, had been there, we would have heard and seen nothing more than shrieking animals and pure primal rage).

Plush sat in the tree, eavesdropping, not sure what he felt. Guilty that Jayden got hurt. Angry at Travis for casting all the blame on him. After all, it was not his fault that the baboons attacked. Yes, he knew he should have scouted the pasture before attempting to steal the cow, but it was almost dawn, and the humans were never seen outside their village at night. He sighed. He didn't hear the rest of the argument below, but he noticed the hunters leaving the forest with gloomy faces, determined but sad. They left the forest and trudged wearily out towards the savannah.

Less than thirty minutes later, however, they were back, shaking their heads and looking angry. Travis stormed up to them and demanded to know why they were back so early and why they had no cow.

"The moon is too bright, and the humans are having some sort of festival. If we even approached the cows, the humans would be able to spot us immediately," said Brandon shamefully.

The starving apes looked unhappy, but most of them were secretly relieved their friends and family were safe.

Plush sat at the top of his tree feeling hungry and grumpy when the idea came to him--the idea that would change his life forever.

He would go to the cow field, kill a cow, and bring it back all by himself! The idea was perfect. He would move much faster alone. Then, he would sneak into the cow field--not before scouting the area. If he were by himself, he might not even spook the cows as much. But this was when he realized the biggest flaw in the plan: how would he get the cow back to the ape forest? Even the smallest cows were very heavy, and he knew he wouldn't be able to carry the body all the way back to the tribe alone. Only seconds passed before he found a solution: he would hide the body in the savannah's grass, cover it with leaves, return to the ape forest, and inform the tribe of the kill. Then *they* would help him retrieve the cow. They would all see he was capable, and, surely, he would be accepted and earn his permanent place into the tribe!

Without skipping a beat, he climbed down the tree, ran to the ape armory, grabbed a spear, and then silently tiptoed out of the forest. Most of the apes were asleep and the ones who were awake paid him no attention; they were too focused on other things like being hungry.

As he stepped out into the plain under the glow of the full moon, he thought he heard someone calling his name. Probably his grandfather. He had to hurry! If his grandfather found out he was missing, he would raise the alarm, and if they noticed the missing spear, they might put two and two together and follow him. He had to hurry! Plush took a deep breath and placed his hands on the ground. Standing on all fours, he closed his eyes and after saying a silent prayer to the ape God, he took off, running fast and stealthily through the tall grass. His limbs beat the ground as he ran, his spear tied to his back with vines. He couldn't see much in the tall grass, but he knew the way by heart. He ran and he ran, not stopping once, until he was close enough to see the pasture.

Plush crept closer and sniffed the air. He could smell the cows. Carefully, silently, he stood up on his toes, his head barely rising above the grass. He could see the village. It was silent now; whatever party had been happening was over, and only a few villagers sat tending to the fires. They were out of earshot, but if the cows panicked they might see the movement in the moonlight and come to investigate. Plush did notice the small cameras placed on the fence posts. But he had no idea what they were and assumed they couldn't be dangerous. He crept up to the far gate and reached out with his hand to unlatch it when SNAP! Plush screamed in pain as sharp metal teeth sank into his right leg, tearing into his flesh.

In the blinding pain, Plush looked down and saw what looked like a metal jaw clamped to his leg. He looked around, biting down to try and stop himself from screaming, though any creature in half a mile would have already heard his yell. Plush looked around and noticed that the ground around him was glinting with a faint silver light that was almost entirely concealed by grass and dirt. "*Traps!*" he thought.

Tears of pain rolled down his cheeks, and as he looked back at the village, he saw two humans rushing down the path towards the cow field. Both were carrying guns. Plush was filled with horror. He tried pulling his leg out of the trap, but the jaws were chained to the ground. The humans had reached the cow field. Thanks to the tall grass, they weren't able to see Plush yet, but they were running around the edges of the cow field, approaching fast. Plush bent down, and using all his strength, pried the metal jaws off his leg. He heard it SNAP shut when he let go. He was about to run back toward the ape forest when he realized the fence line was also surrounded by metal jaws. He couldn't risk stepping on another trap, and even if he avoided all the traps, his cut leg was not going to let him outrun the humans; his only option now was to hide. The humans had split up, each running down opposite ends of the fence. The only way for Plush to escape was to plunge straight into the cow field; he leaped forward, flicked open the gate, and dove into the cow field. The grass in the pasture was even denser than the grass in the savannah. He could barely see a few feet in front of him, but he moved into the middle of the field, having no idea where the humans were but making sure to stay low and quiet.

The two men stopped at the gate. After nimbly stepping over their traps, they opened the gate and crept in. The cows were going mad with fear, running around and smashing into the fence. Big Ben loaded a long thin rifle. Little John did the same, and the two men began looking for Plush.

Poor Plush! He was wincing from the pain of his injured leg as he army-crawled through the field trying not to get trampled by the panicking cows. He had dropped his spear after stepping in the trap, so he was also unarmed. Tears spilled down his face. Why had he been so stupid? Why had he run off by himself without telling anybody? Nobody knew where he was, no one could help him. As he lay on the ground crying like a toddler and holding his injured leg in his hands, he felt a dark presence standing over him. At first he thought it was a cow, but then he heard laughter. He turned around and his heart jumped into his throat. Towering over him was Big Ben. Plush was terrified. He had never been so close to a human before--at least not since his parents' death.

Big Ben raised his rifle but Plush, thinking fast, grabbed at the gun's barrel and angled it away from him. Big Ben tried pulling the rifle out of Plush's grip, and the ape and human had a brief tug-of-war with the gun as Big Ben shouted for Little John's assistance. The tug-of-war continued until a large bull came trampling out of the brush right at Big Ben.

Big Ben released his rifle sending Plush rocking backwards and momentarily dazing him. Big Ben dived to the side and just barely avoided getting trampled. Plush tried to crawl away, but, with surprising speed for a man so large and heavy, Big Ben grabbed at Plush's injured leg. If Plush's leg had not been injured, and he had not been in agonizing pain, he would have ripped Big Ben apart, but the stinging pain was blinding and dizzying. Even so, Plush was determined to escape.He scratched at Ben's face with his claw-like nails. Ben howled and let go of Plush who tried crawling away, but Big Ben jumped forward landing on top of him. Plush screeched, punched, and kicked at the human, but Ben was very heavy and fairly strong. Plush felt Ben's hand grab his injured leg and clamp down on the gaping wound. Desperately, he grabbed Ben's arm and sank his teeth into it. Ben screamed, swore, and cried. He released Plush and once again had to dive sideways as a cow ran past.

Plush crawled as fast as he could, but suddenly he felt a foot hit him in the face, and just as he turned around ready to fight for his life, something flew through the air and whistled into his back. Plush plucked the strange object out of his skin. Squinting, he saw a small dart with a red feather at the end, and suddenly his head began to spin and he had the unbearable urge to sleep--just lay down and sleep.

Plush fought the urge as hard as he could, but it was too strong; he fell to the ground drifting in and out of consciousness. Through blurry eyes, he saw Little John standing over him holding a smoking tranquilizer gun. Big Ben also stood up, picked up his gun, and walked over to Plush, looking down at him. For some strange reason, Plush sensed something familiar about the fat orange-haired human as if he and Plush had crossed paths before. Big Ben raised his rifle in the air and brought the butt of the gun down hard on Plush's face, and the ape remembered no more...

CHAPTER 5
The Council's Decision

Big Ben glared at Little John angrily.

"**Y**OU TOOK YOUR TIME! I NEARLY GOT MY FACE RIPPED OFF BY A MONKEY, JOHN!"

"Sorry, Your Highness," said John sarcastically. "I was trying to not get trampled to death by cows...and, Ben, this is NOT a monkey. It's a chimpanzee, idiot."

"I know that," hissed Ben. He shined a bright flashlight over Plush's body, taking in his small size and the bright patch of white fur on the top of his head. There was something familiar about this ape, but Big Ben couldn't place it. "Wait a minute!" he said.

"What is it?" asked Little John, curiously.

"Remember years back when we hunted those weird-looking apes? When Mr. Winson got his jaw broken?" said Big Ben.

"Yeah. All those chimps had white fur on the top of their heads. Never heard of chimps having white hair on the top of their heads before that raid. Weren't you with Mr. Winson right before those two apes jumped him?" asked Little John. "But why do you care, Ben? That was years ago."

Big Ben shined his flashlight over Plush's forehead, and in the brightness, clearly visible, was a small patch of snow-white fur.

"WOW," said Little John, amazed. "This ape must have been from that savannah. We know at least two escaped; this must be one of them!" Little John said excitedly.

But a frown crossed Big Ben's face. "This ape is young, mid- teens if you ask me. It would have been a baby at the time.

Regardless, we need to take it back to the compound. The Boss will love to hear this."

"Oh, call him Mister Winson, would you? You know he hates being called THE BOSS."

Ben picked up Plush and the two men set off walking. When they reached their Land Rover, they tossed Plush into a small wooden box in the trunk and hammered the lid shut. Quietly, Big Ben and Little John climbed into their car and drove off. The swaying grasses whispered in the wind and the moon gleamed while all the creatures of the savannah slept--from the youngest villager to the oldest ape.

No one knew that Plush was gone. No one knew that at that moment, across the river, the baboon king Bruno was mourning the loss of his son who had vanished some days prior. And no one knew that as Bruno wept, he came to a deadly conclusion:

"Apes must have done this! Those evil apes must have kidnapped and killed my son. CURSE THEM!" And scratching the bleeding bump on his temple where Plush had smacked him with a rock, he called for his messengers. "FLY, FLY TO THE OTHER MONKEY CLANS. TELL THEM WHAT HAPPENED. TELL THE TO ASSEMBLE HERE TO AVENGE THE LOSS OF MY SON. TELL THEM WE ARE GOING TO WAR!"

****

As the sun rose a few hours later, the apes in Plush's tribe awoke and began to go about their daily lives. One group went to the nearby river with big buckets to get water. Another group began searching the ground and trees for roots and small bugs to eat. Plush's grandfather, being about twenty years older than any other ape in the forest, indulged in an extra few hours of sleep.

Around midday, he climbed out of his small nest in the trees. He had noticed Plush's absence but didn't pay it too much thought. He assumed his grandson had been annoyed and angry and had spent the night elsewhere in the forest. "Teen apes," he muttered under his breath. He had a meeting with the ape council that afternoon, and since he was the elder, he knew his presence was badly needed. He would look for Plush after the meeting. Purcellville grabbed his cane and climbed slowly down the trunk of his tree. As he made his way through the forest, he walked on two legs instead of four. He looked more like a man than an ape with his cane. As he passed, some apes called hello, and some stopped to watch; the old ape seemed to emanate authority. But as he walked into the council's clearing, he noticed immediately that something was wrong. The council members were quietly muttering to each other in hushed, panicked voices, and in the middle of the clearing, looking surprisingly and deeply concerned, was Travis. Once he noticed Purcellville, he gave a loud, deep shout, and the muttering stopped. The meeting began. And Purcellville soon learned the reason for their fear.

"According to our bird spies across the river, Bruno, the baboon king, has sent messengers to the other baboon clans; they have come together and seem to be forming a massive army," said Travis.

"We fear an attack is coming soon," said a council member.

"Their numbers have grown from the roughly three hundred monkeys in Bruno's clan to several thousand. If they attack, we will be overwhelmed quickly," said Mucha.

"What say you, Purcellville?" said Travis. "As the elder, I hope you have an answer to our problem."

Purcellville paused, and then said, "Bruno has attacked us in large groups before but never with an army of more than several dozen monkeys. He enjoys hurting us, knowing we cannot swim across the river to attack back. He enjoys watching us suffer, but he has never wanted to wipe us out before; it would bore him. Why would he want to do that now?"

Mucha spoke up, "According to the bird spies, his only son and heir, Bongo, has vanished. Nobody has seen him for almost a week. Bruno believes we are behind the kidnapping."

"The fool!" muttered Travis. "We couldn't have crossed the river unnoticed. We would've had to build a bridge. But when has Bruno ever been smart about anything?"

As usual, they all looked to Purcellville for advice; he was known for almost always having the solution. Purcellville thought and thought, his old brain working overtime. After a while he spoke. "We should send bird messengers to the apes of the northern mountains where the gorillas and the bonobos have united as one tribe. They are greater in strength and numbers than us; they have the strength to help us stop Bruno."

Most of the apes brightened up at this proposal. But Travis, annoyed, butted in, "Even if the apes of the north agreed to help us, it would take them weeks to prepare and just as long to get down here, not to mention the army of baboons in between us."

"What if we agree on a date to attack them, hold them off and buy time until our northern troops arrive? If the baboons don't attack us first, we can attack from the south, distracting them. Then the northern apes will surprise them from the north. Until the northern apes arrive, we will need to hold the forest somehow." Purcellville had finished talking.

"Even if the northern apes agree to help us--and that is a big "IF"--we don't stand a chance against that many baboons. We have roughly eighty apes in this forest, and not all of them are fit to fight," said Travis.

"If you have a better idea, then by all means share it with us," said Purcellville.

Travis glared at him, but then he sighed, "Alright, you win, Purcellville. Mucha, see to it that the messages are delivered to the northern apes. I will begin battle plans. DISMISSED!"

"Good," said Purcellville. "Well, if the meeting is adjourned, I must go find Plush." Purcellville's comment was met with silence. The council members looked scared, as though they were hesitant to speak. Immediately, he knew something was wrong.

"WHAT IS IT?" growled Purcellville. "Has something happened to Plush?"

Travis, looking very annoyed, pointed at Mucha and said, "Explain." Then Travis walked away. Mucha sighed.

"Purcellville, your grandson was seen sneaking out of the forest last night just after the hunters returned from that failed mission. This morning Brandon and his fellow hunters followed Plush's footsteps, and they led them right to the human village. We believe he tried to take a cow by himself."

"And?" said Purcellville, dreading the answer.

"Well, he has not returned, and we believe the humans may have captured him," said Mucha.

Purcellville stood rooted to the spot. He couldn't think. He couldn't breathe. NO! This couldn't be true. This had to be a trick, a prank, a cruel trick! Plush was fine. He was standing behind a tree, ready to jump out and say, "Gotcha!"

Purcellville remembered the previous days' events...Plush's public humiliation...his vow to be accepted by the tribe...and, now, his footprints to the human village... As the true meaning of Mucha's words sank in, Purcellville couldn't see. White fog clouded his eyes...he heard voices...apes shouting his name...but it didn't matter. Nothing mattered. He had failed...failed his daughter...failed his son-in-law...failed Plush. He had failed himself. The old ape felt all the sorrow and trauma of his life at once, and his old heart burst into pieces. His cane fell to the ground. He let out a gasp, grabbed his chest, and fell, landing in a heap on the ground. Mucha screamed and ran to Purcellville's side. He felt his pulse, and his face turned white as snow. Albert Apenstein rushed to Purcellville's side and put his ear to his old friend's chest.

"He is having a heart attack! We need to get him to my infirmary!" he shouted.

With the help of several of his assistants, Albert carried the writhing ape to the infirmary, a small area under a large tree with several moss-covered beds and a collection of wooden and clay cups, pots, and buckets. Gently, they placed him down on a wooden operating table. Albert rushed to a table with multiple clay jars on it. He grabbed a purple liquid, ran back to the dying ape, and with the help of his assistants, forced the liquid down the ape's throat. Purcellville slowly stopped shaking and moaning. His chest began to move up and down slowly. Albert sighed with relief.

A few hours later Mucha stood before the ape council "Purcellville is alive, but he is in a deep, and possibly irreversible, sleep. Healer Apenstien says he has a fifty percent chance of survival. The herbal remedy that Healer Apenstien gave him is experimental and dangerous; if the medicine is not effective, Elder Purcellville will DIE."

CHAPTER 6
The Monkey and the Snake

Plush was lying on a hard stone floor, neither sleeping nor fully awake. He had no idea where he was. He remembered flashes of the last few hours--feeling the car bounce and shake as it drove; being carried, half-conscious, through large metal doors; getting thrown onto a cold stone floor. After that, it had been so dark and quiet that Plush faded back into unconsciousness. Now, hours later, he lay silently, his injured leg throbbing painfully. He eventually became aware of a tickling feeling on his face, and when he reached up to brush it away, he heard a voice speaking in a language that he understood but couldn't place. His eyes were still closed, and he was still only partially conscious.

"Is it dead?" said the voice, raspy and sharp.

"No, it's definitely breathing," said another voice; this one was higher than the first one and sounded much closer to Plush.

"What is it?" said the first voice.

"An ape of some kind. Not a hundred percent sure," said the second voice.

Plush was still half asleep, but he knew one thing. The two voices he heard were NOT human voices; they definitely belonged to animals he recognized, one of them speaking in something vaguely reptilian and the other in something primal. He opened his eyes a fraction and saw it: a large brown furry face, a long jutted snout, and big bulbous eyes. It was a baboon. It didn't notice that Plush's eyes were cracked open. Instinct and adrenaline filled Plush, and he balled his hand into fists. SLAM! His fist flew onto the monkey's face. The baboon jumped back, squealing. Plush jumped up and stood facing the monkey, adrenaline and leg pain surging into him. For a split second, he was sure that the monkey in front of him was Bruno. He was the spitting image of the Baboon King! However on closer inspection, Plush realized his error. Although he was the same color and had the same eyes as Bruno, this monkey was smaller and looked far younger than Bruno.

"Relax, we're not gonna hurt you, crazy Ape," said the monkey. His voice was surprisingly soft and high like that of a very small child. The monkey and ape stood facing each other. They were within inches of each other's height. Plush, keeping one eye on the monkey, looked around and was shocked to see where he was. He was standing in a dark room with very little light except for a small dusty ray of sunlight streaming through a barred window in the far end of the room. It was so dim that he could barely distinguish the large trough filled with brown dirty water in the corner. The walls were also unusual. They were not plastered as one would expect inside a human dwelling; they were reinforced with steel bars built right into the wall. Plush realized he was in a cage, a giant cage the size of a shipping container!

"Where am I?" asked Plush in a panicked voice.

The baboon sighed sadly, "You're in hell, Ape. And this is where you are going to be for the rest of eternity." Then, to Plush's shock and confusion, the monkey burst out laughing; he laughed and laughed. Plush stood watching the monkey roll around laughing like, well, a monkey (maybe this really was hell, he thought). It seemed as though the monkey was never going to stop. Then, he heard a loud HISS.

From behind the monkey, a dry raspy voice said, "Oh, knock it off, Bongo, you stupied monkey. I am trying to sleep."

The monkey--Bongo--stopped laughing and instantly turned pale, shaking with fear as an enormous python with dark green scales and a long forked tongue slithered out of a dark corner, his head rising high into the air. His body was so large and long that, when fully extended, it stretched out over the entire cage.

The terrified Bongo bowed before the enormous snake.

"Please, oh great Peter the Python, please forgive me," said the monkey, his voice shaking and his body trembling. "I was simply welcoming our new cell mate."

It was clear the monkey was terrified of the great snake and Plush could understand why.

"New cellmate?" the snake hissed. And then, his eyes flicked towards Plush. No, not eyes. Eye. The snake's right eye was bright green, but his left eye was just an empty socket. Something was very familiar about that snake, and then it hit him. Could this be the same snake that had tried to eat him when he was a baby? The same snake that had lost his eye after being stabbed by his grandfather years ago? The terrifying creature matched the description his grandfather had repeated so many times over the years--a roughly twenty-foot, African rock python with green scales. A sudden fear gripped Plush: the idea of being trapped forever with a sing-songy baboon and a snake that looked more than capable of murder was beyond depressing. The horrible reality of his situation hit him. He was going to rot here forever (wherever "here" was). He was never going to see his grandfather again or go on the amazing adventures he had always dreamed of. And as Plush slumped to the floor, tears poured down his face. Why had he been so stubborn? Why had he ignored the rules? Why did he feel the need to run off on his own? And why, why, why did the humans take him? Probably not for food; they would've just killed him. Plush didn't know what the humans wanted him for, but he did know that no ape or animal of any kind ever returned after being taken by humans. His thoughts were interrupted by the baboon, Bongo, who sat down next to him.

"You know, I was just kidding about being trapped here forever," said Bongo cheerfully.

Plush wiped his tears with his hand and stared at the monkey. He noticed that Bongo was about the same age as he was, thirteen or maybe fourteen years old in human years.

"What are you talking about?" said Plush.

"Well," said Bongo. "I have only been here about a week, but that python, Peter, he has been in this place for years. He says he knows the way out, but he won't tell me. He says he needs help to escape but won't tell me how because he thinks I would leave him behind, which of course I probably would, if I could." Softly, he continued, "Between the two of us, that snake gives me the creeps, but I need him to escape and get back to my tribe."

"Where are you from?" asked Plush.

"The southern savannah," said Bongo. Plush gasped. Anger immediately surged through him.

"YOU'RE ONE OF BRUNO'S THUGS!!" Plush stood up, glaring daggers at Bongo, who also stood up, shocked.

"You mean you are part of Travis's tribe?" said Bongo.

"YOUR TRIBE IS CRUEL AND EVIL; WE APES ARE STRUGGLING ENOUGH, AND YOU AND YOUR RAIDERS MAKE US SUFFER. WE DIDN'T DO ANYTHING TO YOU!" Plush screamed.

"I had nothing to do with the raids and have never even been on one," said Bongo. "It was my dad, Bruno, who..."

"DAD?" yelled Plush. "THAT MANIAC MONSTER IS YOUR *DAD*?"

The python, Peter, was stirring. "BE QUIET," he hissed, but they ignored him. Plush couldn't believe this sing-song, carefree fool he was trapped with was Bruno's son. The memory of Bruno beating him to within an inch of his life while his thugs stole the cow the apes had worked so hard to get came to mind, and Plush felt blinding anger.

With a deafening roar, Plush launched himself at the monkey. Summoning all his strength, he slammed Bongo against the cage wall, shaking the whole thing. Blinded by rage, Plush sent his fist into the baboon's belly. Bongo crumpled while Plush exploded, exacerbated by the pain from his searing leg wound. He jumped back and flew towards Bongo, but much like his father, Bongo was very nimble and quick. He dodged Plush who collided into the cage wall. Bongo sent a flurry of blows across Plush's face, but Plush was barely dazed. Bongo was clearly not an experienced fighter. Plush was in full rage mode, swinging his long arms at Bongo who retreated to the back of the cell, accidentally stepping on the Python's tail.

With a loud "HISS," Peter the python joined the fray. His enormous tail thrashed around the room, trying to grab the scrambling primates. Bongo and Plush were running in circles around the snake who was so long he could move parts of his body in every direction. Peter felt his scales wrap around one of his prey. Not caring who it was, he opened his fangs in the direction of the primate, intending to rip its head off, but as his gaze fell on Plush, something flickered in the back of his memory. Peter gasped. The memory of a white-haired ape stabbing his eye out came back to him, startling him so much that he completely missed Plush, slamming his own head into the cell door. BANG! The building shook from the collison, and Plush escaped the gripping scales. The snake was dazed. But not for long.

Plush and Bongo resumed their wild chase around the cell, dodging the thrashing scales of the powerful python. Finally, Plush caught the monkey, but his triumph was cut short by the terrible HISS again. He looked up and saw the python's large head flying down at him and Bongo.

BANG! SMACK! POW! CRASH!

The noise had attracted the humans, and as Big Ben and Little John came tearing up the corridor towards the cell, the brawl stopped.

When the two men stopped outside the cell door with tasers and knives in their hands, they saw a very odd sight. In his desperate attempt to capture the apes, Peter the Python seemed to have tied himself in knots; he was lying on the far side of the cell in a tangled green mass that resembled a bow tie. Plush and Bongo were both sitting on opposite ends of the cell, yelling curses and insults at each other. All three of them seemed to be covered in cuts, bruises, and scrapes. Big Ben and Little John didn't know whether to laugh or be angry at the ruckus their prisoners had created.

"You really think it was a good idea to put a monkey, an ape, and a snake in the same cage?" Little John asked.

"Well, we didn't have a choice--we had to send the rest of the cages to Yori's men in Tanzania. They're hunting elephants there, remember? So, unless you want one of them wandering free around the warehouse, there is nothing we can do. Besides, that python learned his lesson the last time he tried messing around," said Ben. The two men laughed and walked away. They reached the end of the dark hallway, turned a corner, and were gone.

Plush and Bongo paused a second and then went back to fighting.

"WILL YOU TWO KNOCK IT OFF? IF YOU EVER WANT TO GET OUT OF HERE, YOU TWO WILL HAVE TO PUT YOUR STUPID RIVALRY ASIDE," hissed Peter.

"What makes you think I would ever work with either of you? Baboons and apes have been enemies for years; and I'm gonna be honest, Peter, but I don't feel completely comfortable putting my trust in the same snake that tried to EAT me when I was a baby," yelled Plush.

"Well, then, we will all rot here. I know how to escape, but I need hands, and, UNFORTUNATELY, I DON'T HAVE HANDS," said Peter.

Finally, Bongo spoke up. "Look, we're all from the same place, and we all want to get back there. We'll just have to work together."

Plush shuddered at the thought of working with two animals that he had very good reason to hate and mistrust. But when he thought about his grandfather, he knew he had to escape. He had to return home, and if teaming up with Bongo and Peter was the only way to do it, so be it.

"OK. Say I agree to work with you. How exactly do we get outta here?" asked Plush.

"I can't tell you everything because obviously I don't trust you, but I will tell you part of it and reveal the rest as needed," said Peter. "First, we need the keys that the fat human uses to unlock this cell. He keeps them on his belt. When they come to feed us later, one of us will need to distract him while another gets the keys. That's the first step."

"But won't he notice the keys have gone missing?" asked Plush.

"I doubt it. They have many spare keys, and they lose them all the time," said Peter.

"Then what do we do?" asked Bongo. "Escape the cell and beat up the humans? Maybe you eat them, Peter?" said Bongo excitedly.

"NO!" said Peter, annoyed. "After we get the keys, we need to destroy the moving-eye monsters on the ceiling."

"Moving eye WHAT?" said Plush, confused.

"The eyes--those moving eyes--that always watch us," said Peter, pointing to a black circular object on the ceiling. "I believe the human call them 'cameras.'"

"So what do we do in the meantime?" asked Bongo.

There was a dramatic pause before Peter said,

"We wait."

Plush sat in the cage, thinking. He couldn't be sure how long he had been here... an hour... a day... a week? It seemed like forever. The only sign of the passing time was the tiny sliver of sunlight that sank beneath the sill of the small window on the wall. Eventually, the sunlight turned to moonlight, and Plush still sat waiting, waiting for the moment the humans would come back and they could get the keys.

"Hey, Ape, they're not gonna be back for hours, might as well do something to make time pass," said Bongo.

Plush stared at him. "Do you even care that you're trapped in a cage being held by humans?"

"Yeah, I do, but I just want to know more about you. I don't even know your name? What is it?" said Bongo.

"My name is Monkey Slayer," said Plush sarcastically.

Plush expected the monkey to get insulted or scared at this, but to his annoyance and shock, Bongo laughed. "Well, that's a dumb name. Your parents must be weirdos!"

"I don't have parents. I am an orphan," said Plush angrily.

"Oh," said Bongo, "so your name isn't really Monkey Slayer?"

"OF COURSE NOT! I WAS JOKING, DUMB MONKEY!" said Plush.

"So your name's Dumb Monkey?" said Bongo, clearly confused.

"NO! IT IS PLUSH, YOU STUPID MONKEY!" yelled Plush, losing his temper.

"QUIET," hissed Peter. This time they obeyed, and Bongo sat right next to Plush and began whispering, "So how did it happen?" asked Bongo.

"How did what happen?" said Plush.

"How did the humans capture you?" said Bongo.

"I don't see how that is any of your business," said Plush.

"Fine, don't tell me, but for me, well..." and he was off talking so fast Plush could barely tell what he was saying.

"...I was walking along the river bank alone looking for termites when I was attacked by a pack of wild hounds. They came out of nowhere and chased me through the tall savannah grass. Finally, they chased me up a tree and surrounded it, so I couldn't escape, and after being trapped for an eternity, a full FIVE minutes, the humans came and shot me with a red feathery dart that made me want to sleep, and, well, I went to sleep and then I woke up and I was in here."

"There. I told you, so now it's your turn. How did you get captured?" asked the baboon curiously.

With nothing better to do, Plush grudgingly told Bongo everything about his life--how he was an orphan, how his grandfather raised him and how he joined the hunters. He also told Bongo about how, after the dry season came, all the herds moved up north the apes began to starve. It was because of this starvation that they had started to raid the humans for food. When he got to the part about Jayden getting shot and the fight with Travis interrupted by the baboon attack, he left out the part about his fight with Bruno; he wasn't sure if Bongo would understand. Plush talked about growing up being an outcast, always being shamed for being different and never really fitting in with the other apes. He told Bongo about trying to steal a cow by himself and getting caught in the trap, and he finally told him about Big Ben and Little John kidnapping him. Plush might have aggrandized the fight scenes a bit, but for the most part, he recounted the events truthfully. And when he was done, Bongo was looking at him, impressed.

"Wow," said Bongo. "You know, Plush, I'm also a bit of an outcast in my own tribe."

Plush stared at him, "You? An outcast? You're the king's son! Surely, you're not."

"It's not that simple," said Bongo sadly. "Sure, being the king's son has its benefits, but I am not like the other baboons. We baboons pride ourselves on being strong, vicious creatures, and I never really had that in me. Also, I am..." he sighed like he was about to reveal something very personal and depressing. "I am the only monkey in the last hundred years who...WAS BORN ALLERGIC TO BANANAS." And with the terrible confession of his chest Bongo burst into tears, sobbing like a baby.

"THAT'S IT? That's what makes you an outcast? Because you have allergies? I thought you were being serious for once," said Plush, now very annoyed.

"I know a mindless ape like you wouldn't understand," said Bongo through his tears. "Bananas are the sacred food of all monkeys. We believe they were given to us by our god, and we believe if you're unworthy of the banana, you're unworthy of life. If I wasn't the king's son, I probably would have been expelled from my tribe years ago."

Plush couldn't help but feel sorry for Bongo. Plush knew what it was like to be laughed at and mocked for something he had no control over; he also understood the shame of living with his grandfather who he could never compete with. Deep down, he wondered if apes and monkeys were more alike than he previously thought.

"How about you, Peter, what's your story?" said Bongo.

Though Peter hadn't spoken the entire time and did not respond to his question, Plush got the feeling that the snake had been listening very closely.

CHAPTER 7
Plans and Parrots

Purcellville lay on a moss-covered bed breathing slowly. Next to him lay Jayden covered in dried blood; he was missing several teeth, and he had two black eyes and a broken rib. Albert Apenstien stood over Jayden washing the dried blood off his face. He was exhausted.

"Two apes in critical condition and in the same day,"

he sighed and went back to work. Suddenly, he heard movement and as he turned, he was shocked to see Purcellville stirring. He rushed over to his sleeping friend's side and checked his pulse--it seemed normal. Albert was just about to return to cleaning Jayden's bloodstained face when he heard the sound of sobbing.

Purcellville was lying there, eyes wide open, sobbing hysterically. Albert was amazed and horrified. The medicine he gave Purcellville should have kept his heart pumping, but only enough to keep him alive; there wasn't enough blood going into his brain for him to be fully conscious, and yet there he was wide awake and crying, just crying. Getting over his shock, the doctor ran back to the old ape's side and looked into his tear-soaked eyes.

"Purcellville, can you hear me?" he asked. Purcellville looked at him and slowly nodded. Albert couldn't believe it. There was no way this was possible, and yet, just as he was overcoming his shock, Purcellville spoke. "Albert, is that you?" he whispered so quietly that Albert could barely hear him.

"Yes, old friend, it's me. Are you okay? How do you feel?"

Purcellville ignored the question and looked around. As if in a dream, he whispered. "Albert, is Plush really gone?"

"I know as much as you," said Albert gently.

Then as quick as Purcellville had awoken, the old ape drifted back to sleep. Albert sighed.

"Rest now my, old friend," he said and making sure Purcellville was stable, he went back to cleaning Jayden's wounds.

****

The ape council was in a panic, screaming and squealing. Among them, Travis stood glaring over a small African gray parrot who he had pinned against a tree trunk.

"WHAT DO YOU MEAN BY THIS?" he roared.

"I...I...I...am just the messenger," squeaked the parrot in fear.

"I was promised a lifetime supply of birdseed from the northern apes if I deliver this letter to a...uh...Misses Travis?"

"THAT IS KING TRAVIS TO YOU, YOU MISERABLE DRUMSTICK! AND WHAT DO YOU MEAN, THE NORTHERN APES WILL ONLY HELP US IF WE LET THEM KEEP THE ENTIRE BABOON TERRITORY? WE NEED THAT LAND MUCH MORE THAN THEY DO, WE HAVE NO FOOD AND LITTLE TO NO WATER. MEANWHILE, OUR SO-CALLED ALLIES ARE UP IN THE MOUNTAINS THRIVING WITH FULL STOMACHS AND NOT A CARE IN THE WORLD, SO TELL ME, DRUMSTICK, WHY DO THEY NEED THAT MUCH LAND? WE HAVE HAD NO FOOD IN ALMOST A WEEK! WE ARE STARVING AND AN ARMY OF BABOONS MIGHT ATTACK AS AT ANY MOMENT."

The parrot was terrified but furious at being called a drumstick and tried again to explain, "The northern kings say they will not help you unless you promise them that you will let them keep the entire baboon land."

"I GOT THAT PART, DRUMSTICK! JUST TELL ME WHY THEY WANT THE ENTIRE BABOON KINGDOM. IT'S ALMOST TEN TIMES LARGER THAN OUR FOREST."

"I don't know," said the parrot. "I'm just the messenger, but I need to know your decision."

"YOU WANT TO KNOW MY DECISION? WELL, HERE IT IS!" And blinded by anger, Travis grabbed the parrot by the neck and with both hands violently twisted it. There was a loud SNAP and the parrot fell limply to the ground dead.

"Really, Travis?" said Mucha. "You can't just go killing the northern ape's messengers." Travis glared daggers at Mucha.

"Oh, just send one of our messengers who looks like this one; they won't notice a thing."

And Travis bent over, picked up the body of the parrot, and took a large bite out of it. Then he turned and tossed it to the ground and walked away. Blinded by hunger, every council member ran at the dead bird, shoving and biting each other to get a mouth-watering morsel of the food as all remnants of a civilized society were gone. They were only apes after all.

CHAPTER 8
Human Food Stinks

"DINNER TIME!"

The voice of Big Ben echoed across the hallway as the two men, both carrying large buckets, came around the far corner.

Immediately, Bongo and Peter fled to the far edges of the cage.

"Remember the plans," whispered Peter. Plush couldn't help but notice the fear in his voice, and again he wondered why the snake feared the humans. He was big enough to swallow a human whole, but there he was, cowering as far away from the cell door as possible. Plush stared at him. As the snake curled himself in a ball, Plush noticed something that he hadn't seen before--something that made him feel sick. On the snake's underbelly, huge scars zigzagged deep into his scales--so deep that much of the skin was missing. It looked like some terrible monster had gouged the flesh out with its terrible claw, but the scars looked old -- a few years at least.

Plush felt something boil inside him.

"How can the humans do this to other living creatures, torturing them for years on end? Death would have been better," thought Plush. He couldn't help but feel pity for the great snake, forced to suffer for years and years with chunks of his skin ripped off, forced to live in endless darkness and pain. It was overwhelming. Plush watched the humans laughing and smiling as they walked up the corridor, and a mixture of anger and fear gripped him. One thing was for sure: he couldn't spend a second more in this place. He had to get out NOW.

He ignored Bongo and Peter calling his name, telling him to get into position. He lay down right next to the cell door, pretending to be asleep. Big Ben and Little John reached the door. They both had buckets filled with some unknown meat, "Parrot, maybe," thought Plush.

Little John inserted the key in the lock, and the door slid open a crack. CRASH!! Little John screamed and lept back in terror as Plush seemed to snap awake. He lunged at the cell door, grabbed it before Little John could close it, and wrenched it all the way open. It happened so fast the humans couldn't react immediately. Plush had leapt outside the cell and was running away as fast as he could.

"PETER, BONGO, RUN FOR IT!" he screamed.

Plush heard shouting and screaming behind him. He turned his head as he raced down the long hallway. He could see and hear the two humans running after him, shouting. He didn't stop. As he turned the corner, he saw a flight of stairs going up. He ran up the stairs, taking them two at a time. When he reached the top, he realized he had made a mistake: the wall across the landing where he thought there must surely be the door turned out to be a dead end. It was just an empty wall. Fear clutched at him as he heard laughing behind him, and he turned just in time to see Little John bring a nightstick down hard on his head. Plush screamed in anguish and fell to the ground in a heap. He heard laughing from the two humans, and then the horrible beating began.

Blow after blow rained down on Plush, each much worse than the last. He curled up on the ground in the fetal position as the two humans kicked and punched him, laughing and shrieking in that horrible human shriek that sounded like a dying hyena. Plush couldn't see through the blinding pain. He cried for Bongo or Peter to save him. He cried for his grandfather. How long was this going to go on for? Pain seared every inch of his body. And then it was over. The beating stopped. Plush lay on the floor moaning as the pain in his body seemed to only grow despite the fact that the beating had stopped.

Little John tied Plush's hands and feet together, though there was no need. Plush made no attempt to escape even as they dragged him down the stairs and threw him back into the cell. He lay there sobbing like a toddler.

"That should teach you some manners, Ape. We don't like animals that break the rules," said Little John, and the two men laughed. Big Ben reached for his keys to lock the cell door, but they were not there.

"Great, I must have dropped the keys when the ape tried to run off," Little John groaned.

"You buffoon! You lose those keys so many times! Wait here while I go get the spare," said John.

And he left the room, returning a few seconds later with another set. They locked the door and walked away, laughing. Plush tried to stand, but he was in too much pain.

"We saved you some meat," said Bongo happily, and he tossed a piece of odd-looking meat at Plush who was so hungry, he grabbed the meat and weakly took a big bite.

"PLAAAAA!!!!" shrieked Plush, and he spat the meat out of his mouth. It was DISGUSTING.

"What is this garbage? It tastes like fried pheasant and old oil!"

"Yeah, I felt the same way when I first got here, but it's all we get, so you might as well eat it," said Bongo.

"It's an unnatural horrible creation that humans call 'fast food,'" said Peter harshly.

Plush sighed with shame, and he said hoarsely, "I'm sorry. It was really dumb of me to try to run off like that."

"You *should* be sorry! The plan was for you to pretend to be unconscious while Bongo and I fought in the back of the cell. They would have come in to break us up and you were supposed to get the keys," hissed Peter angrily. "Because of you, we lost a chance to get the keys. The humans are going to be more careful now--we're never getting out of here!"

"I wouldn't be so sure about that," said Bongo, and to the utter bewilderment of both Peter and Plush, he held up a small set of silver keys.

"WHAT?! How on earth did you get those?" asked Plush.

"When you ran off, the humans left the door open, and as they ran after you, I followed them. When I got to where you were, they were so busy beating you up, they didn't see or hear me walk up behind them and take the keys off the big man's belt. After that, I just walked back here." He finished talking and sat down and began playing thumb wars with his tail.

"YOU WERE FREE??? WHY DIDN'T YOU HELP ME?" said Plush with a loud roar.

"I thought it was part of the plan," said Bongo, confused.

"WERE YOU EVEN LISTENING WHEN WE MADE THE PLAN?" said Peter, losing his mind.

"I was busy playing rock, paper, scissors with my tail when you guys were making the plans. I heard something about "Plush" and "fighting," but my tail was cheating, and I was trying to explain the rules to him," said Bongo like he thought it was a reasonable excuse.

"Never mind. We have the keys! What do we do now, Peter?"said Plush.

"Our next move is to destroy the cameras; there is one in this cell right there." He pointed his tail at the left corner of the cell's ceiling and at the weird-looking camera aimed at the door.

"There are three more like it outside the cell," said Peter.

"Wait, I don't understand," said Plush. "How do the moving- eye monsters work? They're not animals, so what are they?"

"Human Dark Magic, if you ask me," said Peter. "They are mysterious creatures, humans. They don't look like much, but they are powerful beings. Their creations tear this world apart. They build monsters that they ride around on, they even build machines that they can fly around in the air. They are demons! They violate every law of nature we know, even gravity. What are they?"

Peter finished talking although he didn't seem to be talking to anyone--it was as if he was just thinking out loud.

"So we could escape right now!" said Bongo eagerly.

"My dad, Bruno, always said waiting is pointless, patience is pointless... or maybe it was my tail who said that? I can't remember."

"I DON'T CARE WHAT YOUR TAIL SAID, BUT IF YOU DON'T START TAKING THIS SERIOUSLY, I AM GOING TO EAT YOU, BONGO," roared Peter, losing his temper completely. "We can't escape yet," he continued more quietly. "This place is crawling with humans. If you didn't know, we're inside a massive human settlement. If we try to escape, we will be spotted. We have to wait until nightfall. Even if we can get out of this building, there are humans everywhere. We must wait.

Peter, who looked exhausted, amazed Plush. How much did the snake know about this place! When he asked him how he learned all the information, Peter simply said, "I listen."

Excitement filled Plush's mind. The idea of finally getting out of this place was overwhelming, and for the first time since he arrived, he felt happy.

CHAPTER 9
Doctor Nile

The next few hours went by very slowly. Plush sat watching the tiny ray of sunlight peeking through the small window in the cell. He was thinking very hard. In the distance, he heard the sounds of the two humans deep in conversation.

"It's your turn to get groceries. Go grab some food, John."

"All you think about is food. No wonder you're 260."

In the distance, Plush heard the two human voices erupt into a violent battle of name calling and swearing. As he listened, he tried to discern the babble of yells and shouts that emitted from them. He tried to copy what they said, repeating their shouts in whispers. After a few hours of this, he seemed to understand some of what they were saying. For example, he heard the words "no" and "buffoon " more than once, and as he listened, he realized he was beginning to understand more and more what they were saying.

"I CAPTURED HIM! HE WOULD HAVE GOTTEN AWAY IF IT WASN'T FOR ME," said Little John, fuming with anger.

71

"WELL, I WAS THE ONE WHO DISCOVERED HE WAS ONE OF THOSE WHITE-HAIRED RUNTS! I SHOULD GET TO TELL NILE WHEN HE ARRIVES TO TAKE BLOOD TESTS," said Big Ben, equally angry.

"YOU JUST WANT TO TAKE ALL THE CREDIT AND GET MR. WINSON TO PROMOTE YOU OR SOMETHING. I WAS THE ONE WHO SEDATED HIM. IT WAS ME!" said Little John.

Plush couldn't completely understand what they were saying, but he got the impression that they were talking about him. He kept listening, but the argument seemed to have stopped, and Plush heard a new voice down the hall, a strange, high-pitched Irish accent that sounded almost like it was coming from someone rather small--like a young child. This confused Plush, and he continued listening, hoping to at least get the tone of the conversation.

"Well, Ben, John, I don't have long. I leave for England in a few hours, and I hope you have an important reason for delaying my flight," the new voice said.

"Yes, Nile, we found one--one of the weird-looking apes Mr. Winson has been searching for," said Big Ben excitedly.

"Really?" said Doctor Nile slowly with a hint of disbelief. "Bring it to the operating room. I will need to run a few blood tests."

"Ok, but I warn yah. This one is troublesome. He has tried to escape before, and he got really close, too," said Big Ben.

"Regardless, I still need blood samples, so get him over here and hurry. I do not have long."

"You don't believe us, do you?" said Little John angrily.

"Well, it has not been the first time you two have claimed to have a certain species in your inventory and been wrong. Remember that time you claimed to have found a long lost DODO BIRD, BUT

WHEN I EXAMINED THE ANIMAL, IT WAS JUST A DEFORMED CHICKEN?" said Nile.

"YOU'LL SEE --- WAIT HERE. I WILL GO GET THE APE," said Big Ben, fuming.

Plush heard a movement down the hall, and around the corner came Big Ben and Little John. They reached the cell door and opened it. Peter and Bongo both retreated as far from the door as they could. Big Ben grabbed Plush, jabbed him with the taser--a clear warning not to resist--and strapped a leash around his neck. Plush was still hurt from the beating and didn't dare struggle as they pulled him out of the cell and walked down the hallway. They reached the stairs where Plush had been beaten, and Little John grabbed a rope hanging from the ceiling and pulled a small trap door that Plush had not noticed before. It opened, and a long, wooden ladder was lowered down. Little John went up first, and Big Ben pulled Plush up the rickety ladder. They emerged in a well lit office with sofas, desks, and computers all over the room.

"Ah good, bring him to my operation table," said Doctor Nile. Plush had never seen a human like Doctor Nile before. His first thought was that Nile was a young human, not fully grown (when in fact Nile was over 40 years old). Dr. Nile was barely 5'2" in height, had short blonde hair, and wore a long white lab coat. Nile was also incredibly skinny, giving him the appearance of a lean twelve-year-old. The only thing that looked adultish about him was the few wrinkles on his face. He also wore a pair of large, round-shaped glasses that magnified his eyes, making them look much larger than they really were.

Big Ben heaved Plush onto the operating table and, using a pair of leather straps, Ben and Little John tied Plush's arms and legs to the table. Plush was too scared and hurt to resist.

"See? Look at his forehead. He has that weird white spot,"

Little John said excitedly.

"Yes, I see that, but I need blood samples to confirm ITS identity," said Dr. Nile.

He approached Plush and looked him over, taking in the injured leg and the numerous bruises on him. Suddenly, Nile erupted in anger shouting and pointing at Plush's leg.

"WHAT THE HELL DID YOU DO TO THIS THING ? IT LOOKS LIKE IT WAS MAULED BY A PACK OF WOLVES!" said Nile.

"That ape tried to escape, and we had to teach it a lesson," said Big Ben, smugly. Nile spun around, stepping toward Big Ben and Little John.

"YOU FOOLS! LOOK AT THIS THING! YOU'VE BEAT TO WITHIN IN INCH OF ITS LIFE! YOU COULD HAVE KILLED IT, AND LOOK AT HIS LEG! IT'S PURPLE AND SWELLING. OH GOD, IT'S ALREADY INFECTED. I'LL HAVE TO TREAT IT. I WILL MISS MY FLIGHT BECAUSE OF YOU BUFFOONS!! JUST WAIT TILL Mr. WINSON HEARS ABOUT THIS!"

Nile's face was turning redder every second--not out of pity for Plush but rather anger at the damage done to his research. His immediate rise in temper shocked Big Ben and Little John, but not as much as it shocked Plush. The stunned ape couldn't believe what he was hearing. He knew what Nile had said. Somehow, he understood not only the tone, but the meaning of their conversation; it was as clear as daylight. Plush understood Human.

CHAPTER 10
Second Thoughts

N g'ombe Miji was in chaos. Villagers crowded in Chief Akida's house, shrieking with anger. The town council was trying to explain the situation, but the many voices bickering with anger, fear, hatred and pain made it almost impossible to be heard.

"WE SHOULD PRESS CHARGES. THEY SHOULD BE ARRESTED!" yelled one villager.

"I KNOW YOU'RE UPSET. YOU HAVE EVERY RIGHT TO BE, BUT PLEASE CALM DOWN," said Akida, trying to make his voice heard.

"CALM DOWN? CALM DOWN? THOSE SWINES, BIG BEN AND MINI JOHN, OR WHATEVER THEIR NAMES ARE, LEFT ABOUT A HUNDRED BEAR TRAPS OUTSIDE THE FAR FIELD. WHEN WE WENT OUT TO FEED THE COWS THIS MORNING, A BUNCH OF US STEPPED IN THEM AND GOT OUR LEGS MAULED!" roared the villager.

Akida looked around the room and saw that almost all the villagers had heavily bandaged legs; some could barely walk.

"NOT TO MENTION THE FACT THEY LEFT OUR PASTURE GATE OPEN. ANY OF OUR COWS COULD HAVE WANDERED OFF," said another villager. The shouting rose higher and higher.

"I KNOW, I KNOW, BUT--AT LEAST THE COWS HAVE STOPPED VANISHING," said Akida.

"YEAH, THEY STOPPED DISAPPEARING, BUT WE'RE STILL BEHIND ON WORK, AND MOST OF US CAN BARELY WALK. THE MANAGER OF THE EAST AFRICAN MEAT PROCESSING PLANT IS NOT PLEASED WITH OUR LATEST NUMBERS. IF WE DON'T PICK UP THE PACE, THEY MIGHT STOP BUYING OUR COWS. WE'LL BE BROKE!"

The shouting grew louder and louder. Every villager knew if they lost their business, they would have to abandon their village--the village where their ancestors had lived for thousands of years. Farming cattle was all they knew. Since the savannah was legally government property, if they could not afford to pay real estate taxes, they would lose their livelihood, their homes, everything.

****

The apes' forest was in an almost identical state of panic as the humans'.

"WE'RE DOOMED. EVEN IF THE NORTHERN APES ARRIVE ON TIME, WHO IS TO SAY THEY WILL KEEP THEIR PART OF THE BARGAIN? THEY MIGHT JUST TAKE OUR LAND, TOO!" The voice of Mucha rang through the clearing,where the ape council stood trying to appease the crowd of angry chimpanzees that stood before them.

"THE BABOONS COULD ATTACK AT ANY MOMENT AND KILL US ALL! WE DON'T HAVE THE NUMBERS TO REPEL AN ATTACK OF THAT SIZE, AND WE CAN'T EXACTLY LEAVE THE FOREST. WE CAN'T OUTRUN THE BABOONS ON FOOT NOW THAT THE DESERT BABOONS HAVE JOINED THEM. THEY CAN TRACK US FROM ALMOST ANYWHERE ON EARTH; THOSE DESERT SCAVENGERS HAVE NOSES BETTER THAN HUMAN HUNTING HOUNDS! WE HAVE NOWHERE TO GO! WE CAN'T RUN, WE CAN'T HIDE AND WE CERTAINLY CAN'T FIGHT THEM. ALL WE CAN DO IS WAIT," said Travis, shaking with anger.

All around him the apes' screeches grew louder and louder.

"Where is Purcellville when you need him?" said Travis under his breath.

As far as they were aware, Purcellville was still in a comatose state. According to Apenstein, the medicine would wear off in about a week's time, maybe a little longer. They couldn't be sure; all they could do was wait.

****

A few miles to the north and across the river, Bruno the baboon king sat on the edge of the river bank thinking. Memories of Bongo playing in the river kept coming back into his mind. "So carefree, so happy," he thought. His hatred towards the apes was matched only by one thing: his hatred for himself. He blamed himself just as much as the apes. Truth was, he felt if he had not raided the apes and had not hurt them for his own pleasure, they wouldn't have taken his son. And if he had raised Bongo to be stronger, maybe he wouldn't have been so easy to capture. His thoughts were interrupted by the arrival of a messenger monkey.

"King Bruno, the other monkey kings wish to speak with you," said the messenger.

"CAN'T YOU SEE I AM BUSY? WHAT DO THEY WANT?" said Bruno.

"Not sure--they told me to get you. I think they're having second thoughts about joining you," said the monkey.

"SECOND THOUGHTS? WHAT DOES THAT EVEN MEAN?" yelled Bruno, and not waiting for an answer, he charged away from the river towards a massive crater. It was very deep and as wide as a football field. No plants grew inside, just dry, cracked dirt, and it was also full of baboons.

Bruno's clan were the grassland baboons. They were the largest clan, and the most numerous out of the local troops. Next, there were the forest baboons or mandrills. They were the largest baboon species in the world; they were mostly black but had pink and orange faces. The mandrills lived in the forest just north of the grassland and just south of the northern mountains, where the gorillas and pygmy chimpanzees or bonobos lived. The mountain troops were now moving south and meeting little resistance as almost the entire baboon population had gathered in Bruno's territory.

Next, came the desert baboons; they were mostly black and they lived in the desert northwest of the savannah. The desert baboons were smaller in size and less numerous than the other baboon clans. However, they had an advantage that the other baboons did not; they had the best tracking skills out of any primate. Their noses could compete with that of a bloodhound.

Though they had their differences, the various troops were usually on good terms. They all shared a love of bananas and they all shared a hatred of apes, though until now, only Bruno's clan had actually done harm to apes. Bruno, furious at learning that his fellow monkey kings were hesitant to proceed with his plan and wipe the chimpanzees off the map, stormed into the crater in a mad rage.

"YOU ARE ALL TRAITORS TO MONKEY-KIND! HOW DARE YOU QUESTION MY PLANS. ACCORDING TO THE TREATY OF THE TAILED PRIMATES, WE ARE ALWAYS TO COME TO ONE ANOTHER'S AID AS I HAVE DONE A MILLION TIMES FOR YOU," roared Bruno.

"WE NEVER BETRAYED YOU. WE JUST WANT TO SPEED UP THE PLANS. WE FOREST BABOONS WERE UNDER THE IMPRESSION THAT WE WERE COMING SOUTH TO DESTROY AN APE FOREST--NOT WAIT AROUND FOREVER. WE WANT TO ATTACK NOW! WE HAVE THE NUMBERS, WHY DON'T WE ATTACK NOW?" said the mandrill king.

"Yeah. We want to attack them now. We're getting bored just waiting," said the desert baboon king.

"I KNOW YOU WANT TO ATTACK THE APES NOW, BUT LISTEN TO ME," said Bruno. "WE NEED A FEW MORE DAYS TO GATHER OUR TROOPS. I WANT EVERY BABOON THAT CAN FIGHT HERE BEFORE WE ATTACK. IT'S NOT LIKE THE APES ARE GOING ANYWHERE," said Bruno.

"But why do you want every baboon in our clan? You already have more than enough monkeys to destroy the apes?" said the desert king.

Bruno took several deep breaths to calm himself, and then he smiled a crooked grin that revealed bloodstained teeth.

"I want to destroy the apes slowly. I want them to watch in horror as thousands of baboons surround their forest and close in on them. I want to hear them scream for mercy as I avenge my son." Bruno finished talking and stared at the other kings, challenging them to disagree with his plan. "We will wait until the full moon next week. The full moon is a symbol of good luck to all monkey kind, and it would also have been Bongo's fourteenth birthday. I want to honor my son by avenging him on the day he was born. I want to give every baboon the chance to finally destroy our ancient enemies for good."

King Bruno stared at his fellow kings, waiting for their response. The other two kings had a quick muttered conversation under their breath, and then they both stared at Bruno and screamed in unison: "WE'RE IN!" .

****

Doctor Nile had finished cleaning Plush's leg wound, patching up his bruises, and taking lots of blood tests. Plush didn't know just how long he sat there being poked and prodded by needles and syringes. He lay without resisting. When Doctor Nile wiped his injured leg with alcohol, it stung and burned, but somehow Plush knew it was doing more good than harm.

"You said this ape is a trouble-maker. He didn't even need anesthesia. Most chimps would have tried to rip my face off, but this ape hasn't moved at all. I am deeply impressed. Where did you find this specimen?" said Doctor Nile.

"In a cattle village out east," said Big Ben.

"Well, you two may be correct about this ape. I will need to analyze his blood work first, but I think you might have hit the jackpot," said Dr. Nile.

He walked over to the desk and put a few drops of Plush's blood under a microscope. After about five minutes of Nile shuffling around the desk doing this and that, he stopped working and turned to Big Ben and Little John, and sighed.

"Oh, great. My electronic microscope is out of battery."

"Can't you just charge it?" said Big Ben.

"I left my charger in my lab in Britain. It's one-of-a-kind. Keep this ape safe. I will need to take the blood samples to Britain to analyze them properly."

Doctor Nile began to pack his equipment when a loud ringing sound came out of his pocket. Nile pulled out his cellphone, and his eyes lit up when he saw the number calling him. He snapped "OUT" at Big Ben and Little John who looked annoyed but left the room as ordered, slamming the door behind them.

Nile answered the phone and held it up to his ear. Someone on the other end was speaking quite a lot, although all Push could hear was faint static and the rumbling of his own stomach. He hadn't realized how hungry he was. He had not eaten anything in several days.

"Look, I know, Mr. Winson, I am taking this seriously. Yes, I realize we're not supposed to discuss business over the phone. Yes, I know the CIA is monitoring your landline. Yeah, and your cells. Yes, I set up the end-to-end encryption and scrambled my location data. No, they can't trace my location. I know, but you need to hear this: I think we found one, a Captiosus Simia. No, I am not a hundred percent sure. I need to get back to my lab and analyze its blood samples. I know, yes, okay. Look, I will be on the next flight to England and meet you there. Okay, I thought you should know."

"FOOOOD...."

Doctor Nile looked around, searching for the source of the noise. His eyes fell on Plush. He had almost forgotten Plush was in the room. But apes can't talk; maybe he just imagined it.

"Look, Mr. Winson, I know, but I don't think that would be possible. They won't let me take an ape on a plane. We'll just have to be patient."

"FOOOOOOD..." This time the voice was stronger, more insistent.

Nile looked around. He definitely heard something, and this time it sounded like it was coming from Plush.

"FOOD," said Plush in perfect English.

There was a short pause, and then, "AAAAAAHHHHHHH!"

Doctor Nile screamed, jumping back in fear and amazement.

"I...I am gonna call you bbback...." he stuttered and hung up the phone.

Nile approached Plush. In all his years as a scientist, he had never seen anything like this before. His ears must have deceived him, but soon the voice spoke again, and this time, Nile saw the ape's mouth move, forming the sounds.

"FOOD," said Plush, getting impatient. Maybe he wasn't saying it right. He tried again. "FOOD, GLOOD, BLOUD!"

Doctor Nile opened his bag and pulled out an energy bar; he tore it open and approached Plush. Being a man of science, he immediately began constructing hypotheses to explain how this could be possible. Maybe the ape just sounded out the words he heard humans speak. But when Plush said "FOOD" again and licked his lips, Doctor Nile knew that somehow this ape knew what he was saying. As if in a trance, he stood over Plush who was still strapped to the table. He held the bar over Plush's face and lowered the bar into Plush's mouth. Plush, overcome with hunger, wolfed down on the snack, as Dr. Nile watched in disbelief.

****

"KEEP THAT APE LOCKED UP! NEVER TAKE YOUR EYES OFF IT! OH, AND PUT A TRACKER ON IT. KEEP IT SAFE; I WILL BE BACK IN A FEW WEEKS. OH, AND GIVE IT SOME REAL FOOD–FRESH FRUITS OR RAW MEAT. MR. WINSON WANTS IT ALIVE AND UNHARMED, SO ABSOLUTELY NO BEATINGS. GOODBYE." And Nile walked out of the facility,slamming the door behind him and leaving a bewildered Big Ben and Little John.

Nile, shaken by the unlikely turn of events, had not told them about Plush talking; he had only said that he had to leave and that they were to keep Plush safe and unharmed. The two humans took Plush back to his cell and locked him inside. A few minutes later, they returned with a large collar made of wires and rubber which they strapped around his neck.

Bongo and Peter wanted to know what had happened to him, so Plush told them some of it, leaving out the part about him speaking and making it seem like Doctor Nile had just given him a treat. Bongo fell for it, but Plush caught Peter's eye, and he was pretty sure the snake knew he was not telling them something.

CHAPTER 11
A Rift in the Plan

Plush spent the next twenty minutes trying to get the collar off. He didn't know what it was, but it was very tight and uncomfortable. Unfortunately, no matter how hard he tried, it wouldn't come loose. His attempts to get the collar off were interrupted by the snake.

"Well, since you're back, we need to go over the plans," hissed Peter. The snake raised himself to his full height (which was impressively high). "We wait until night. Then, we will need to act fast," said Peter. "Plush, you and Bongo will need to climb the walls and take out the cameras as fast as you can. We should have a few minutes before the humans realize what is happening. Once you two take care of the cameras, we will need to get the trapdoor open and lower the ladder. It's the only way that leads to an exit, and we will have to navigate a maze of shelves and boxes. Don't worry. I know the way to reach a large metal door that leads outside to the wider human settlement."

"How do you know the way?" asked Plush suspiciously.

"You dare doubt me, Ape? For your information, the two humans running this place used to take me to gladiator fights for their amusement. We went to another building where they would make me fight other animals, but after Mr. Winson got wind of it, they stopped."

"Who is this Mr. Winson?" said Plush, confused and curious.

Peter didn't speak immediately; he paused for some time.

"Mr. Winson is the human in charge of this operation. He is the only thing that frightens those thugs, Big Ben and Little John. He is their ruler, their master, their superior. I have only seen him once before. He is a horrifying, unnatural, nightmarish creature--an amalgamation of human cruelty and unholy existence."

"What does that mean?" said Bongo, scratching his forehead with his tail.

Peter hissed at being interrupted but continued. "He is somehow alive despite missing one of his legs and one of his eyes. He has replaced his missing body parts with metal appendages of unimaginable horror. He is the walking devil, the living dead, the..."

"Can you go back to the part about escaping? This is scaring me," said Bongo who was holding his tail in his hands and shivering with fear.

"Anyway, the fights served their purpose, and I remember the way out. The metal doors lead to a large open area where humans walk around freely and ride in the mechanical creatures they call cars."

"Are you sure you still know the way?" said Plush. "If it has been years, you might not remember..."

"I KNOW THE WAY OUT, APE!! NOW SHUT UP AND LISTEN, AND IF YOU INTERRUPT ME ONE MORE TIME..."

"I don't mean to interrupt," said Bongo, "but even if we get out of here, how on earth are we going to get back to our savannah? None of us knows the way."

Plush and Peter stared at Bongo. They realized they had been so busy working on a plan to escape the prison that they didn't even think about how they would get back home.

"We'll worry about that after we get out of here," said Plush.

"Maybe we could ask a bird for help. They might know the way."

"BUT FIRST WE NEED TO GET OUT OF HERE, SO SHUT YOUR OVERLY-SIZED MOUTHS AND LISTEN UP!" yelled Peter, overlooking the fact he had the largest jaw of the group.

Hours passed, and they went over the plan again and again. Peter and Plush made sure Bongo knew exactly what to do. After interrupting Bongo's game of thumb wars with his tail for the fifth time, he was finally able to recite his part of the plan without getting it wrong. So they waited.

Finally, the faint sunlight through the barred window was slowly replaced by soft moonlight. Peter the Python slithered to the cell door and sniffed the air. "They are NOT close, let's go..."

Bongo gave a squeal of joy and ran around the cell, bounding up and down the walls.

"SHUT UP!" yelled Plush and Peter at the same time. Then they realized that they had just shouted as loudly as Bongo.

"Great, you stupid monkey, now we have even less time to get out of here, " said Peter, hissing quietly.

"Do you think they heard us?" said Plush to Peter.

"Plush, all of Africa probably heard that! Let's just hope they don't come to investigate."

Plush and Bongo got into positions: Plush under the camera in the cell and Bongo facing the door with the key ready to unlock the door.

"Now," hissed Peter. And Plush lunged at the wall, scrambling up it so fast the camera didn't even register him. His arm grabbed it and pulled it out of the wall with ease, but as Plush jumped down the wall and landed on the ground, his injured leg screamed with pain, stinging so badly and unexpectedly that he gasped and stumbled.

"What's wrong?" asked Bongo, who wasn't even looking at Plush but was busy trying to find the right key to put in the keyhole. Finally, he tried the last key on the chain and got it right. The door clicked and slid open.

"Yeah, first try!" yelled Bongo. Plush and Peter both stared at him.

"Do you even know how to count?" said Plush, exasperated.

The three of them rushed out of the cell and hurried down the dark, windowless hallway. Bongo jumped from one side of the wall to the other, grabbing the many cameras and pulling them out of the wall. Finally, he finished, and together the three of them hurried up the stairs until they reached the landing with the trapdoor. Bongo had to stand on Plush's shoulders to reach the rope to lower the ladder. Plush tried to ignore the ever-present stabbing pain in his foot. The ladder dropped down, and then they realized they had a problem: how on earth would Peter get up the ladder?

"We'll have to carry him," said Plush, looking panicked. Peter hated that idea, but they had no other option; they had to leave now or the humans would catch them. So Bongo and Plush heaved the body of Peter on their shoulders and began to climb the ladder--Plush went first, with Bongo right behind him. Plush, panting from the weight of the snake, had to use one hand to climb and the other to keep Peter from slipping off his back. He was almost at the top, when disaster struck. CRASH! As Plush stepped on the final rung, his injured leg slipped, and in his panic, he let go of Peter. The great snake fell with a hiss, crashing against the ladder and causing it to splinter into pieces. Bits of wood flew everywhere. Plush lost his grip and fell right on top of Bongo and Peter. Bongo lost his grip, and together they all landed in a heap, banged up and bruised. Peter tried to move, but in doing so, tangled himself even more.

Big Ben and Little John had been playing poker when they heard the noise. They jumped up, raced to the opening, and peered down the trap door only to see a monkey, a snake, and an ape all tangled in a giant knot. Little John laughed and tried to climb down but the broken ladder wouldn't hold his weight, and he fell right into the pile of animals. The next few minutes were very absurd. Big Ben carefully lowered himself down onto the landing and charged the tangle of snakes and primates.

THUD! Plush and Peter tried to fight the humans; the humans tried to grab the apes; and Peter, who was caught in between, tried to slither into a standing position but slipped. The mass of scales collided with the struggling primates, which caused all of them to go crashing down the stairs back into the hallway. Bongo had fled to a corner and was covering his head crying, "NOT THE FACE! NOT THE FACE!"

WHAM! CRASH! POW! SLAM! WHAP! Somehow, Big Ben and Little John got the upper hand. Big Ben pulled a concealed knife from his belt, and Little John drew a pocket taser. And just like that, it was over. All their hard work, all their planning, gone. The three animals were shoved back into their cage, locked into their cell, and forced to hand over the keys Bongo had stolen.

"WE HAVE TRIED TO PLAY NICE WITH YOU ANIMALS," yelled Little John.

"YOU'RE GOING TO ROT IN THIS CAGE FOR THE REST OF YOUR STUPID MEANINGLESS LIVES," said Big Ben.

"WE'RE GONNA TURN YOU INTO MEAT--ALL OF YOU!" said Big Ben angrily.

"Nile said not to hurt the ape; our DEAR cousin Winson wants him alive and unharmed," said Little John.

"WHY? WHY ONE EARTH WOULD ANYONE WANT THAT APE ALIVE AND UNHARMED? IT LITERALLY TEAMED UP WITH A SNAKE AND A MONKEY!" said Big Ben who looked on the verge of losing his mind. Both humans were bleeding badly and sporting multiple bumps and bruises.

"I DON'T KNOW WHY THEY WANT IT ALIVE. IF I HAD A SAY, I WOULD TIE THEM ALL TOGETHER, BIND THEM TO LARGE STONES, AND THROW THEM IN THE RIVER," said Little John.

"I WOULD LOVE TO DO THAT, TOO, BUT THAT MONKEY IS ALREADY UNDER CONTRACT TO A ZOO IN EGYPT, AND THE APE--FOR SOME REASON--IS WANTED BY MR. WINSON. WHATEVER. COME ON, WE NEED TO GO BUY A NEW LADDER."

The humans left but not before giving Plush, Bongo, and Peter a good shock with their tasers. Plush sat in the corner of the cell holding his injured leg sobbing--both from the pain in his leg and the pain in his mind. Peter curled up into a ball and did not speak; he didn't even have the heart to blame Plush and Bongo for the failed attempt. Even Bongo looked depressed. They had failed. Not only would the humans triple their security, but they had lost the keys to the cell. After a while, Peter uncurled himself and slithered up to Plush.

Then, to Plush's horror, the silence of the quiet, depressing room was broken by the roar of the snake.

"YOU DID SOMETHING WHEN THAT HUMAN DOCTOR EXAMINED YOU. YOU'RE HIDING SOMETHING!!! WHAT DID YOU DO? HE WAS TELLING

THE OTHER HUMANS TO KEEP A BETTER EYE ON YOU AND TO NOT HURT YOU. WHY???"

"I...I...I don't know what you're talking about. They were just cleaning my injured leg," said Plush, trying to look confused.

"DON'T LIE TO ME, APE! I HAVE BEEN IN THIS CAGE FOR YEARS! I CAN UNDERSTAND HUMAN SPEECH. I KNOW YOU'RE HIDING SOMETHING. WHAT ARE YOU NOT TELLING US? I SMELL GUILT AND SECRECY IN THE AIR!! TELL ME NOW!!" screamed Peter the Python. Plush decided to tell them the truth. There was no point in hiding it anymore; they were trapped here forever.

"I spoke to him...I was so hungry, and I knew how...I somehow just knew."

"KNEW WHAT?" yelled Peter.

"I knew what to say! I knew how to talk to them!"

"YOU'RE TELLING ME YOU CAN SPEAK HUMAN? THAT'S IMPOSSIBLE! I HAVE BEEN HERE FOR YEARS, AND I CAN DISCERN SOME OF THEIR WORDS, BUT I CAN'T SPEAK THEM. YOU HAVE BEEN HERE...WHAT? A FEW DAYS? AND YOU CAN MAGICALLY SPEAK HUMAN?"

Plush stared at the ground, and Peter realized Plush was telling the truth. Peter was not sure whether to be impressed or angry; he decided on anger.

"IF WHAT YOU'RE SAYING IS TRUE, THEN YOU PUT ALL OF US IN EVEN GREATER DANGER. IMAGINE WHAT HUMANS WOULD DO IF WORD GOT OUT THAT THERE WAS A CHIMPANZEE THAT COULD SPEAK THE HUMAN LANGUAGE? I SHOULD HAVE KNOWN BETTER THAN TO TRUST A CHIMPANZEE...MINDLESS CREATURES," said Peter.

"MINDLESS CREATURES? AND THIS IS COMING FROM A SO-CALLED CHIMP-EATER WHO HAD HIS EYE STABBED OUT BY AN OLD APE WITH A STICK?"

"YOU DARE INSULT ME? CURSE YOU, APE!" screamed Peter, and he lunged for Plush, hissing with rage. Plush also lunged forward at the snake, determined to cause Peter as much pain as he could. Peter's head flew at Plush; Plush dodged him and sent his fist into Peter's face. Peter hissed with pain and swung his tail at Plush. The snake's long tail flew across the floor and lashed out at Plush, causing him to fall onto the large stone floor. Bongo was screaming. Plush was roaring. Peter was hissing. Peter, who had Plush tangled in his large strong scales, tightened himself, his scales closing around Plush.

Peter thought about his life before the humans captured him; it seemed like a distant dream. He remembered being free, happy even. He remembered when he used to be a strong young snake, when he could devour an entire zebra whole. But then, he remembered that night when the ape had stabbed out his eye. Peter the Python squeezed his scales tighter, crushing Plush. "I HAVE WAITED YEARS TO FINALLY TASTE APE FLESH," he growled.

"RAHHHH!!" Plush screamed and thrashed, trying to break free. Plush felt more anger than he had ever felt in his life. Anger at Peter, anger at the humans, anger at EVERYTHING. A blinding rage built up in his body, and Plush--at this moment--didn't care if he lived or died. All that mattered was causing this snake as much pain as he possibly could. Plush opened his mouth and bit down on Peter's scales, his teeth sinking into the snake's flesh. Peter screamed in pain and released Plush; Plush flew at the snake and sent his fist into the snake's face again and again. Plush didn't even know his own name, so blinding was his fury. He struck again and again at the snake. Peter was shocked at Plush's surprising strength, but he was ready. His long tail lashed at Plush, causing him to fly across the room and crash against the wall.

Peter sighed. He turned and lay down thinking he had won; however, as he lay there, he heard Bongo scream, and he turned just in time to see Plush, who was clinging to the barred ceiling, come crashing down on him. Plush landed on Peter's head and without thinking, he wrapped his long arms around Peter's neck. Peter thrashed about, trying to knock Plush off, but Plush seemed glued to Peter's neck. Peter felt his neck tighten; he was going to lose consciousness soon if he didn't do something. With the last of his strength, he flew at the wall, causing Plush to slam against it head first. Plush slumped unconscious and, at the same time, released Peter's neck. The python was free, but he, too, was knocked out. The two animals fell to the ground both still as stones.

CHAPTER 12
Percy the Parrot

It was several hours before Plush came to. He sat up, his head badly bruised. Sunlight was peeking through the small barred window. Plush looked around. Bongo sat in a corner arm wrestling his tail. Peter was lying in a heap curled up and silent. For a split second, Plush thought Peter might be dead, but then he saw that the snake's chest was rising and falling slowly. Plush felt terrible. His body ached everywhere. He tried to stand, lost his balance, and fell. Bongo helped him up and looked very confused.

"What were you fighting about?" he asked.

"None of your business," said Plush.

"Well, what do we do now?" asked Bongo.

"What do you mean?" said Plush.

"I mean, how do we escape?" said Bongo.

"Bongo, there is no escaping. Forget it."

"Don't you want to get back home?" said Bongo.

"We tried to escape. It's pointless. Just forget it," said Plush.

Bongo turned and walked away. Plush returned to his corner and tried to sleep, but he couldn't. Now that he had calmed down, he realized that Peter had an understandable reason for being angry. I was so stupid, Plush thought. Why on earth did I speak to a human? Now the human would tell others, and people would be amazed. They would want to study more apes. They would start hunting apes, and that would put his entire forest in danger. The stress was extremely tiring. Plush was about to doze off when he heard something.

"Apparently, the chimpanzee tribe down south is going to war with a baboon clan. Yeah, the baboon king Bruno said the apes kidnapped his son Bongo."

Plush sat up. The voice was coming from outside the small window. Plush climbed up to it and looked around. The speaker was a large African gray parrot perched just outside the barred window. It was speaking to a small crowd of pigeons.

"Anyways, the chimpanzee king Travis has asked the northern apes for help. He is in a terrible mood. Apparently, the ape's elder Purcellville had a heart attack or something and is in a coma," said the parrot.

Plush gasped in horror.

"HEY, YOU! WHAT ARE YOU TALKING ABOUT? WHAT HAPPENED TO MY GRANDFATHER?" said Plush, panicking. The flock of pigeons looked at Plush and scattered, flying away in every direction.

"WAIT! COME BACK!" said Plush, but they ignored him, and soon they were all gone. Plush sighed and was about to climb down when he heard a voice.

"Hey, what's your problem, Ape? You interrupted the best part," said the parrot. Plush realized that the large bird had not flown away and was still standing on the window glaring daggers at Plush.

"YOU KNOW IT'S RUDE TO INTERRUPT SOMEBODY?" continued the parrot.

"Please...just tell me what happened to the elder, Purcellville, and what do you mean *war*? And what about the northern apes? I thought they hated Travis."

The parrot stared at Plush, "What's it to you?" he said.

"I am from that savannah. The elder ape is my grandfather. Please, just tell me what's happening," said Plush, pleading.

The parrot looked Plush up and down and squawked something in bird language that Plush didn't understand.

"Who are you?" asked Plush.

"The name's Percy, Ape. But more importantly, who are you? What is your name?" asked the parrot inquisitively.

"It's Plush, but that's not important, just tell me what is happening at the..."

The parrot cut Plush off and looked up and down the alleyway.

"If you're really from the southern savannah, what on earth are you doing in Nairobi?" said the parrot.

"I don't know what Nairobi is, but I was kidnapped by humans a few days ago," said Plush.

"Kidnapped by humans? DEAR ME! You really must have set them off," said Percy.

"Can you tell me what is happening in the savannah or not?" said Plush, getting annoyed.

"I am afraid I cannot--goodbye," said the parrot and to Plush's horror, Percy took off flying away.

"WAIT! COME BACK! WHY CAN'T YOU TELL ME?" screamed Plush.

However, as soon as the bird had flown out of Plush's view, he was back again, laughing his head off. Plush was horribly reminded of Bongo and turned around making sure Bongo hadn't died and been reanimated as this bird. However, Bongo was still arm wrestling his tail and paying no attention to Plush or the bird. Plush turned back to the bird; it was still laughing. A mixture of anger and hunger rose up in Plush. He seemed to be watching the laughing bird in a daze and had an overwhelming desire to grab it, bite it, **eat** it. Plush was on the verge of acting on his instinct when the bird stopped laughing and spoke.

"So, you want to know what's been going on back in the savannah down south?" said Percy.

Plush seemed to snap out of his trance and sat up, eagerly. Percy laughed and sat down. Plush heard him mutter under his breath, "Crazy ape. Well, he might make a better audience than a bunch of pigeons."

"Well, Ape, it all started about two weeks ago when the baboon king Bruno discovered his son Bongo was missing," said Percy. At these words, Bongo stopped playing with his tail and his ears perked up.

"Anyway, Bruno believes apes were behind the kidnapping, and even though the apes said they didn't do it, Bruno has been massing a huge army of monkeys and is planning on exterminating the chimpanzee forest," said Percy.

"And what do the northern apes have to do with any of this?" asked Plush.

"Well, from what I was told, the chimp king, Travis, sent emergency messengers to the northern ape tribes, and the gorilla and bonobo kings agreed to come south with their tribes and surprise attack the baboons from the north," said Percy.

Plush was shocked.

"The northern apes have helped us in the past, but they are devious apes! Even Travis should have known better than to ask them for help. They are sly masters of trickery; they only help if they get something out of it. And besides, they're very mean. They never join our slap chats or join our social mayhem."

"So you don't think the northern apes will help the chimps?" said Percy.

"Well, according to ape law, they have to, and they would never go back on their word. But they will change their word. They're probably going to wipe out the baboons and then just take over the ape forest and make us all become vegetarians." Plush shuddered at the thought.

Then Plush remembered the reason he had been so desperate to talk to the parrot. "And the ape elder, Purcellville, what happened to him?" said Plush.

"Well, from what I was told, he had a heart attack after his grandson Plush was killed by humans," said Percy. "Wait--you're Plush." Realization dawned on the parrot's face but was interrupted when Bongo sneezed behind him so suddenly Plush jumped in surprise. Plush had almost forgotten that Bongo and Peter were still in the room.

"He survived his heart attack and is in a coma, but the rest is Nonya," said Percy .

"What's a Noneya...?" said Plush, confused.

"None of ya business," said Percy, and to Plush's rage the small parrot once again burst into laughter. So did Bongo. Plush stood there annoyed, surrounded by two morons. Percy suddenly stopped laughing and looked at Bongo in amazement.

"BONGO, BONGO THE BABOON?" said the parrot in awe.

Bongo also stopped laughing, and his eyes seemed to sparkle with joy.

"PERCY THE PARROT? I THOUGHT I WOULD NEVER SEE YOU AGAIN!" And Bongo ran up the wall and pushed Plush out of the way. When he reached the window, the bird and monkey began some secret handshake (though neither of them used their hands, mainly because Percy didn't have hands, and Bongo preferred his tail).

"Do you two know each other?" asked Plush.

"I used to be a messenger for Bruno's clan a few years back, but I retired. The commute from my nest to the baboons' territory was too much for me."

"What are you doing this far north?" asked Bongo.

"I was visiting my cousins. They live in this area," said Percy.

"HELLO, BONGO!!! WERE YOU LISTENING? YOUR FOREST IS GOING TO BE WIPED OUT BY THE NORTHERN APES," said Plush.

Bongo's face darkened and a look of terror appeared in his eyes.

"Percy, do the baboons know the northern apes are going to attack?" asked Plush.

"I don't think so. The baboons are focused on attacking the ape forest. I only realized the northern apes were coming when I was flying up this way a few days back and saw them passing through the forest baboons' territory," said Percy.

"How did the baboons miss an army of apes marching through their territory?" said Plush.

"Well, most of the baboons are camped out in Bruno's territory, and the few that remain are probably not focusing on the northern border. Besides the apes are very secretive; they only travel at night and they hide during the day," said Percy.

"If they're hiding so well, how do YOU know they're moving south?" said Plush suspiciously.

"Well, a few days ago, I was flying a red-eye, and I stopped to rest in a large tree in the forest baboons' land and found it was full of gorillas, so I hid and listened to their conversation. They are going to launch a surprise attack on Bruno's kingdom. They said they would arrive in ten days' time, but that was two days ago," said Percy.

"NO! We have to warn them! My dad is only attacking the apes because he thinks the apes killed me. We need to escape!! I can get my dad to call off his attack, and YOU, Plush, can get the northern apes to call off their surprise attack," said Bongo, panicking.

Plush puzzled over this new information. Could they get back to their savannah before the baboons attacked his forest or the northern apes surprise attack? But how would they escape from this prison?

"Look, we would still need to break out of here," said Plush.

"And we don't have keys to the cell anymore, and who knows how long it will take to get another pair of keys," said Plush sadly.

"I don't think keys will be a problem," said Bongo.

And to Plush's amazement and bewilderment, Bongo once again held up something--a small ray of sunlight illuminated a single silver key.

"HOW on earth did you get that?" said Plush gaping.

"Oh, well, yesterday when we tried to escape right after we unlocked the cell, I took this key off the keychain. It looked tasty, and I tried to eat it, but it was too hard, so I kept it in my mouth sucking on it. When the humans got the keychain back. I guess they didn't notice the one key missing," said Bongo, shrugging.

Plush couldn't believe that a dumb monkey who spent his time playing thumb wars with his tail had accidentally gotten the one thing they needed to get out of there. For a split second, Plush felt hope, but it was only for a moment.

"Ok, say we DO get out of here? We still don't know the way back to the savannah," said Plush.

"Oh, that won't be a problem, ape. I know the way by heart," said Percy happily.

"Ok, say we do escape this place, and we know the way back home. We still might not make it back home in time. Percy, how long will it take for us to get back home?" said Plush.

"Well," said Percy, "It usually takes me a few days of flying, but since you guys will be walking, it will take longer--a week, maybe longer. I'm not sure. I have never walked the journey before."

"WAIT!" said Bongo. "I have an idea! Percy, why don't you leave now and fly back and tell my dad that I am still alive and that the apes did not kidnap me!!" said Bongo, hopping up and down.

"That could work," said Plush, thinking.

However, Percy was shaking his head and frowning.

"What's wrong with you?" said Plush.

"It's just that I don't think Bruno would believe me. He is blinded by his anger, and a noisy bird telling him his son is alive but imprisoned in a cage with a smelly ape and a half dead python might just make him angrier. The last time a parrot made Bruno angry, the monkey king made a delicious meal of parrot pizza for dinner," said

Percy, and he shuddered. "Even if I warn the apes, I don't see it making a difference. They already told Bruno they had nothing to do with Bongo disappearing, and Bruno refused to listen. He won't believe us unless there is proof, and the only way to get proof and save both of your tribes is for you two to escape from this human civilization and get back to your savannah." Percy paused and then said, "Oh, I just remembered something..."

Plush and Bongo stared at him.

"I am not sure if it is too important, but Bruno is going to attack on the full moon this month, the same day Bongo was born. Bruno believes wiping out the apes on his son's birthday is a good way to get revenge," said Percy.

"The full moon--that's only six days from today!" said Plush.

"I don't think we can make it in time even if we leave today. It's still a long journey, and you guys are probably weak from being in captivity," said Percy sadly. All three of them looked at the ground in defeat.

Then from right behind Plush a dry hissing voice said,

"They won't make it in time."

Plush whirled around. He was face to face with Peter the python. "What do you want?" he said angrily.

"They won't make it in time, Ape. Weren't you listening? The northern apes will arrive eight days from today; the baboons will attack your forest in six days, The northern apes will arrive two days after your forest is attacked," said Peter.

The snake was not threatening Plush or trying to upset or panic him; he was simply explaining the facts.

Plush couldn't believe he was going to lose his entire tribe. No! He couldn't. He wouldn't.

CHAPTER 13
THE MAZE OF DEATH

"**P**ercy, is there any way we could make it back to the savannah in six days?" asked Plush.

Percy thought, "Well, if we leave tonight and travel quickly, ...MAYBE," said Percy.

"Okay, we have to leave now. We don't have time to make a plan. Percy, wait at the exit. There is no point staying at the window; you can't help us until we're outside anyway. Bongo, give me the key; we're getting out of here right now!" said Plush.

"NOW WAIT, JUST A MOMENT," roared Peter. "You will need my help navigating the upper levels of this place; it's a maze. Oh, and one more thing: IT'S BROAD DAYLIGHT. IT IS NINE O'CLOCK IN THE MORNING. THERE ARE HUMANS EVERYWHERE!"

"We don't have a choice. Come with us now, or we leave you behind," said Plush.

Peter thought about it, and then he sighed. "I guess we have nothing to lose. OH, EXCEPT OUR LIVES!"

"Is that a yes?" asked Bongo.

Peter stared at them; his one eye seemed to see into their souls. Finally, he nodded, "Yes, it's a yes."

Plush, Bongo, and Peter rushed down the hallway. The cameras had not been replaced yet, so all that mattered was being as quiet as possible. They reached the trap door and were pleased to see a new metal ladder in place of the wooden one. Carefully, Plush and Bongo slowly lowered the ladder. Bongo went first; he climbed up to the top and put his ear to the trap door.

"I don't hear anything," he said. He opened the trap door and climbed back down.

Plush and Bongo heaved the enormous snake up the ladder. It was difficult as Plush's leg was still injured, but Bongo offered to go first, much to Peter's displeasure. Finally, they reached the top and climbed into the office where Plush had spoken to Doctor Nile. They carefully closed the trapdoor and, as quietly as possible, crept to the only door in the room.

"Remember to be quiet and watch where you step; this room echoes," said Peter.

Plush stepped forward, reached for the door, and opened it. The next room was huge. It had a high, dark ceiling. Unlike the small well-lit office they had just left, this room had no lights. Instead, it was full of towering shelves that reached the ceiling. It was a massive warehouse. The three of them entered the room, carefully tip-toeing through the maze of aisles.

"You sure you know where you're going?" whispered Plush.

"Yes, I do...be quiet. The humans could be somewhere nearby," said Peter.

They kept moving. Plush tried to keep track of time, but it seemed impossible to tell how long they had been in there--an hour, a day?

Plush was about to consider climbing the shelves to find the exit when they turned a corner, and Plush could barely stifle a scream. He clamped a hand over his mouth in horror. Unlike the other aisles, this one was lit; several lamps cast dark shadows on the wall, and Plush felt his blood turn to water.

There were bodies everywhere: ape corpses hung from the ceiling, their legs and arms chained to large hooks. The bodies had been there a long time, but they looked almost normal. It seemed as though they had not decomposed at all. They were chemically frozen in time, looking the same as the moment they had died. Plush fell to his knees. He couldn't move, talk, or look away from the apes that stared back with dead blank eyes.

"Plush, we have to leave," said Peter.

"Plush, the humans are going to be back any moment. We have to go," said Bongo.

Their words meant nothing to Plush. He had caught sight of two bodies at the end of the hallway--the bodies of a male and a female ape. They looked faintly familiar to Plush, who focused on the small patches of white fur on their foreheads. He knew who those apes were or who they once were. His brain was rushing, trying to process his emotions. Fear? Anger? Grief? But it was impossible. Plush couldn't take his eyes off the two apes: he was staring into the lifeless eyes of his parents.

His eyes teared up, and finally his mind and heart were able to find the emotions he felt. He fell to his knees, crying and sobbing. Somehow, he looked more like a human than an ape as he lay there, terror and horror in his mind. This wasn't natural, thought Plush. No ape should have to feel pain like this. It was the kind of pain no animal could feel. It was human pain--sorrow beyond sadness, anger beyond hate, fear beyond horror.

Plush remembered the first rule that the tribe taught to ape toddlers whenever they talked about humans: "No animal ever returns after being taken by humans, and no one ever knows what happened to them." But Plush knew. Plush realized all the apes who had been abducted came here to this nightmare prison where apes were killed and hung like trophies as if they were nothing.

"Plush, we have to go now. We need to hurry! If we don't leave now, our tribes will die," said Bongo.

Bongo's words seemed to rock Plush back to his senses. He turned and stared at Bongo, unable to say anything.

Bongo grabbed Plush and pulled him down the aisle away from the terrible trophies. Plush couldn't move; he couldn't think; all he knew was that Bongo half dragged him down the hall until they reached a bend. They kept moving, aisle after aisle. Plush kept his eyes on the ground, too scared to see what else might be on the shelves. Finally, they turned a corner, and there it was: a large door only a few meters away.

Peter was shaking with excitement. "That's it! That's the exit! That's the way out!"

Bongo sat Plush down and walked up to the door. He was about to open it when he jumped back. Plush had heard it, too--voices. Human voices.

"Quick! Run!" yelled Peter.

Plush didn't need telling twice (Bongo did). When he was finally able to comprehend the gravity of the situation, he grabbed the petrified Plush, and pulled him around the corner, back up the aisle, down another, and around another corner. They finally stopped. Bongo was panting, and Peter was hissing. They waited, not daring to make a sound. In the distance, they heard Big Ben and Little John walking down an aisle not far from where Peter, Plush, and Bongo were hiding. The human voices echoed through the warehouse, getting closer and closer until the two men passed down the aisle right next to where the three animals were hiding. The voices carried down the halls growing fainter. Bongo breathed a sigh of relief and leaned back against the shelf to catch his breath.

CRASH! The noise echoed around the room, bouncing off the walls and ceiling. Bongo had accidentally knocked a metal pipe off the shelf, and it had fallen onto the hard stone floor.

"Oh, no..." muttered Peter, fear rising in his voice.

The humans had stopped talking; they were quiet.

"Hey, did you hear something fall back there?" said Little John.

The three animals huddled together, not daring to move; they knew the humans were listening for more sounds.

Finally, Big Ben spoke, "I think the rats are back. I'll lay some traps out later."

The human voices became fainter and fainter. But Peter and Bongo (Plush was still dazed and unable to think or move by himself) waited until they heard the office door close.

"Hurry, we don't have much time; they will be onto us; we probably only have a few minutes! We have to hurry! I can't spend another second in this Maze of Death," said Peter.

It took a while to find the door again. They tried retracing their steps, but they had been running so fast that they completely forgot where they were. It took a dangerously long time but eventually they found it.

They rushed to the door and opened it; they were about to step through when they heard the loud, terrible screaming. It was not a scream of fear, not a scream of pain. It was a scream of anger, of blinding rage.

"BEN, COME QUICK!!! THEY GOT OUT! THEY ESCAPED AGAIN--THE APE, THE MONKEY, AND THE SNAKE. THE CAGE IS EMPTY!" It was Little John; he had gone down to feed the prisoners their daily meal of spoiled fast food and discovered the door wide open and the three occupants missing.

Bongo, Peter, and Plush didn't wait to hear more; they rushed through the door, and Bongo slammed it shut behind them.

The three animals couldn't believe it. They were finally free.

CHAPTER 14
Peter's Story

Sunlight beat down on their heads. It was blinding. The three animals were standing in a narrow, empty alleyway. On both sides, enormous brick buildings rose high into the air.

"Well, it took you long enough; you look very pale in this light. When was the last time you three saw sunlight?" said a voice. It was Percy.

The parrot was sitting on top of a dumpster. He looked very bored. Clearly, he had been waiting for them for a while.

"Well, no time to delay. We need to get going." said Percy cheerfully.

Plush felt his fear lessen; now that they were away from that terrible warehouse, he felt calmer. It was harder to be scared of something dark and creepy outside in broad daylight, surrounded by his companions. In their excitement, the four animals rushed out of the alley, but their excitement was immediately replaced with terror.

They had burst out of an alley into a busy, crowded city street filled with humans. Humans walking on sidewalks, humans crossing the streets, humans walking their dogs, and humans there driving cars up and down the road. It might have seemed like an everyday scene to you or me, but to Plush and his friends, it was a nightmare even more terrible than the room with the ape bodies.

At the sight of a monkey, an ape, and a snake rushing out of an alley, all the humans stopped and stared, wholly baffled by the three random animals who had just appeared out of nowhere.

Plush felt terror at seeing over a hundred humans staring at him. He panicked and did the first thing that came into his mind. He spoke.

"Hello, all humans," said Plush, a near-perfect Human, though in his panic, he mixed up his words and sounds, so what came out was more like, "Hell, all humans."

Of course, the sight of a creepy animal yelling "hell" was very shocking, and these humans acted like all humans do when a scary talking animal swears at them.

"AAAHHH!!!!!" The humans scattered, stampeding away. Cars crashed and people shoved each other aside as they fled in all directions. Soon the street was empty. Plush, Peter, Percy, and Bongo stood rooted to the spot.

"Why are they running? I just said hello!" said Plush, confused.

"They must have been scared of something?" said Bongo.

"Of course not; humans are fearless creatures who know nothing but hate and cruelty," said Peter.

"There must be a horrifying monster or some scary animals running around this city! We should get out of here--FAST!" said Bongo, looking around nervously.

The group set off running down the street. Percy went first, flying ahead of the group and leading the way. Then came Bongo, who ran like, well, a monkey on all fours. Next came Plush, who was still a little slower because of his injured leg, and finally came Peter, who was surprisingly fast for a snake and did an excellent job of keeping up with the rest of the group.

Towering buildings flew past in a blur. Had Plush not been so shaken from the horrifying experience in the warehouse, he would have stopped to admire the advancement of human technology. Up ahead, Plush saw that the entire street ahead of them was filled with hundreds of people all shouting a common call.

It was a protest for a political movement called SAVE THE DUCKS, and blocking all the roads were crowds of people waving signs and chanting in unison "SAVE THE DUCKS SAVE THE DUCKS!" The crowd was so caught up in their chant they didn't notice the crazy group of animals charging towards them.

"We can't go this way, turn back," said Plush who was horrified at seeing so many humans shouting what he interpreted as "SAVOR THE DUCKS!"

"Okay," said Percy. "Let's cut across the road."

But as the group turned around, Plush's sharp eyes spotted two familiar figures running down the road behind them; it was none other than Big Ben and Little John.

"WE CAN'T GO THAT WAY EITHER! WE'RE TRAPPED!" yelled Percy who had no problem flying over the crowd, all of whom completely ignored him.

As Bongo, Plush, and Peter rushed forward into the crowd, someone yelled, "AHHH! SNAKE!" and people began to run around in every direction bumping and crashing into each other. Other humans, unaware of the animals, still chanted "SAVE THE DUCKS!

113

SAVE THE DUCKS!" It was pure chaos as Plush, Bongo, and Peter rushed through the crowd, finally bursting out the opposite side of the swarm and running away through the streets. Plush glanced back through the riot they had just created and was glad to see no sign of Big Ben and Little John. Sighing with relief, he turned forward and followed Bongo.

As they reached the city's edge, Plush saw massive mountains in the distance--their way home. Humans continued to scatter in every direction as they passed. They were almost out of the city when Plush happened to look back, making sure Peter was still behind him. That's when he saw them.

Far in the distance, fighting their way through crowds of panicking people, were Big Ben and Little John; they were both carrying guns. They pushed their way through the crowd by kicking people's shins, shoving them out of the way, and even threatening one man at gunpoint. Plush suddenly found a new burst of energy and soon the group reached an open area where the buildings stopped and the ground went from gravel to dirt.

****

Plush collapsed against a tree, exhausted; behind him, Bongo and Peter were in the same shape. They had been running almost nonstop for over three hours; they had run, slithered, and flown out of the city and deep into the surrounding mountains. The hills were dense with trees and forests making running difficult, but there was food! More food than Plush and Bongo had seen in weeks: tropical fruit trees, sweet grasses, and some insects. Plush and Bongo were omnivores; they helped themselves to mouthfuls of fruit and bugs. Poor Peter, however, was a carnivore and could only eat meat.

Percy seemed the only one among the group who was not physically drained; he was circling them in the air and talking nonstop. "WOW, you guys really must hate that human city! I have never seen animals run like you just did! If you keep this up, we just might make it back in time."

"Where do we go next?" asked Peter.

"Well, you guys look like you need a rest, so I think we wait a few hours and then continue moving after sunset; We should reach the creek by midnight, and then it's about a day's hike to the river."

Plush wanted to protest. On one hand he was tired and knew he needed rest, but on the other hand, how could he rest with such overwhelming thoughts from the day's events? Slowly, he laid down and closed his eyes with one thought comforting him. For the first time in what felt like eternity, he felt true hope.

****

Big Ben and Little John rushed around their warehouse, grabbing things off the shelves and stuffing them into bags. They grabbed guns, ammunition, and food; they packed everything from net guns to sedatives. Little John even threw a bow and several arrows into their old '93 Land Rover. They had not heard Plush scream, "HELL ALL HUMANS," and were unaware of the ape's mysterious speaking ability.

"We're never gonna find them. They are probably halfway across the mountains by now," said Little John miserably.

"John, you idiot," said Big Ben grinning. "We have a tracker on the ape, remember? (Back on page 113.) It's connected to our phones. We know exactly where to find it."

****

Bongo and Percy were having a VERY loud conversation; Bongo was munching on his fiftieth fruit of the day when he happened to look over at Plush. The poor ape was sitting against a tree trunk staring at the ground, his eyes drifting, and he seemed only half awake.

He had been unable to fall asleep and had taken to sitting quietly and ignoring his companions, all except Peter who seemed overly-excited.

"Hey, Plush, want a mango?" said Bongo.

Plush did not respond; he just kept staring at the ground. Bongo and Percy looked at each other confused.

"Hey, Plush, you alright?" said Bongo.

No response.

"Hey, Plush! HEY, PLUSH!"

"Be quiet," hissed a voice. Peter the Python had slithered up behind Bongo and Percy.

"I was just asking if he wanted a mango," said Bongo defensively.

"Give him a break; he is under a lot of stress. You know what he saw in that warehouse. That nightmare is still hurting him," said Peter, out of earshot of Plush.

"He looks okay to me--just tired," said Percy.

"Ooo, I know what will cheer him up," said Bongo.

"Let's have a fruit fight!"

"No, no, you fools," said Peter.

"He needs space from you two; the poor ape is going to remember that maze with bodies for the rest of his life," said Peter. "You two stay here. I will talk to him ALONE."

"What are you going to do, try and eat him again?" said Bongo, looking suspiciously at Peter.

Peter ignored the monkey's remark and slithered away from Bongo and Percy, and headed towards the distant ape.

Plush was sitting quietly. His brain felt numb like it was not sure what emotions to make Plush feel.

"Hey, Ape, mind if we talk?" said Peter.

Plush did not say anything; he grunted and stared at the ground. Peter sighed.

"Look, Ape, I am so sorry for what you had to see in that warehouse. I can't imagine what you must have felt...." Plush cut the snake off as he stood up, glaring into the serpent's large vertical pupil.

"YES, YOU'RE RIGHT. YOU CAN'T IMAGINE WHAT IT FEELS LIKE. YOU ARE A SNAKE; YOU ARE A SOLITARY ANIMAL. YOU DON'T HAVE A FAMILY. YOU DON'T KNOW WHAT IT IS LIKE TO CARE ABOUT ANYTHING BUT YOURSELF, SO IF YOU ARE HERE TO TRY AND CHEER ME UP, SAVE YOUR BREATH. THE ONLY PERSON I HAVE LEFT IN MY LIFE IS LYING ON HIS DEATHBED. I SHOULD BE THERE WITH MY GRANDFATHER, BUT I AM NOT; I AM MILES AWAY IN THIS STUPID FRUIT-FILLED PURGATORY!"

Plush felt tears forming in the back of his eyes. He expected Peter to lash out and attack him, but when he turned to face the snake, he saw that Peter had tears in his eye, too.

"You're right, Ape," said Peter.

"I don't know what it feels like to care about somebody or to have somebody to care about me..." he sighed. "But Plush, you're not the only animal who has suffered here. I might not know what it feels like to lose somebody, but I know pain, I know fear, I know hopelessness, I know suffering."

Plush had a strong urge to argue and fight, but the words Peter said seemed to sink into his mind, and as he stared at Peter, his entire view of the snake changed. Plush no longer saw a scary, vicious evil serpent; he saw an old, scarred creature who had suffered endlessly for years. Plush had been in that human prison for a little more than a week, and it was the worst time of his life. Peter had been in that place for years.

When Plush was two or three years old, he had asked his grandfather what had happened to the snake who had tried to eat him. His grandfather had told him that word from bird messengers had reached the ape forest and that the snake had been captured by humans a mere week after losing his eye. Plush couldn't believe the snake had been in that hellish cage for almost TWELVE YEARS. Plush realized he had been so eager for "freedom" from the tribe all his life; he did not realize he already had it. He turned to face the snake and saw that Peter was crying.

"I am a monster," said Peter.

Plush wanted to say something, but he couldn't find the words, and it seemed like Peter was talking to himself more than he was talking to Plush. Peter, however, adjusted himself so his drooping head was facing Plush.

"You know, Ape, when you first arrived in the human prison, I wanted to eat you. I wanted to hurt you after what happened to my eye. I thought all apes were heartless monsters, and when I learned you were related to the ape who took my eye, I thought I could finally get revenge." Peter sighed. He spoke with emotion and pain in his voice.

"I was planning on using you and Bongo to escape and then eating you and getting revenge on your grandfather for taking my eye..."

Peter took a deep breath and stared directly at Plush, his head now level with Plush's.

"I was so blinded by rage I thought only about what he did to me, not why he did it to me. But now I see it's because you care about each other; after our failed escape attempt, we had both given up. I thought we were never getting out of there, but you were the one who inspired us to try again. It was not anger or rage that got you moving again; it was love, your love for your grandfather, your only family. You became so focused on escaping and getting home when you learned he was in trouble. I realized my entire view of the world was wrong. I am the monster, not you, not apes. I am no better than the humans; I'm a villain."

Peter finished talking, and he curled up into a ball, he sniffled and a single tear ran down his remaining eye. Plush felt utterly overwhelmed. He tried to process what Peter had said. He couldn't believe this was the same Peter the Python who had been so aggressive towards him when he was first imprisoned. Now this same snake was crying and calling himself a villain.

"No, you're wrong," said Plush. Peter looked up.

"Ape, you don't have to lie; I was going to kill a bunch of innocent baby chimpanzees, including you. I don't deserve to be free. I should be back in that cage. I ruined your life. I am responsible. I..I'm sorry."

"NO," said Plush. "It was the humans who killed my parents, not you; it was the humans who kidnapped me, not you; it was the humans who tortured me, not you. You might have made mistakes. Hell, maybe you *were* a monster. But now you have a second chance. We both do. If you want to make up for what you have done, you can. I made many mistakes, too, but we're free now."

Plush couldn't believe what he had said; he felt like a wise old ape, like his grandfather, and to his further surprise, Peter actually smiled.

"Thank you, Ape," said Peter. He paused, then said,

"Thank you, my friend."

Plush was about to respond when suddenly CRASH!

Plush screamed in shock as something brown and furry fell in a heap from the tree above him.

Plush soon learned that the furry thing was Bongo. He had been hiding in the tree eavesdropping on their conversation but had lost his footing and fell.

"I TOLD YOU TO STAY AWAY AND LET ME TALK TO PLUSH ALONE," roared Peter.

Bongo got unsteadily to his feet and, catching sight of Peter and Plush, angrily staring at him, he screamed, "IT WAS PERCY'S IDEA!".

CHAPTER 15
Apes Can't Swim

Peter and Plush didn't talk much for the next couple of days. The group found the mountain creek quite easily and followed it downstream, stopping to rest every couple hours. According to Percy, they were making great time and had about a one out of a MILLION percent chance of getting back in time (which Bongo thought was great odds). There were not many animals in the semi-tropical forest which surprised and frightened Peter, but Percy assured him it was migrating season and most of the animals that lived here had left for the season.

Plush wanted to talk to Peter more, but Peter was being distant from the rest of the group. Bongo and Percy were oblivious; they spent all day chatting and laughing, sharing stories and talking about old times. Plush tried to engage in conversation with the monkey and parrot, but his mind kept drifting away from discussions about fruits and allergies to the nagging questions in his mind.

How on earth could he understand and speak the human language? One of the many mysterious things about humans was that no animal could ever understand or speak their language--it had always seemed to be magically unlearnable. However, the humans also couldn't understand any animal language either, so the fact that Plush, a runty ape who had only been in human presence for about a week, could suddenly understand and speak it was baffling. Even parrots like Percy, who could sound out human words, didn't really understand it.

When Plush told Bongo about his thoughts, the monkey didn't really seem interested; Bongo seemed to think that the reason Plush could speak and understand humans was simply because Plush was a weirdo.

"But that's not a problem because I am a weirdo, too," comforted Bongo. "I guess it's just something else we have in common," he shrugged, and to Plush's deep annoyance, Bongo and Percy began to sing. It was not a typical tune; it was a bird song, which means it sounded something like this…

"SQUEAKITY SWAK SWEE SWAK SSSSWAAAAK!"

Bongo and Percy sang like this for a very long time; Plush was much too overwhelmed with anxiety to pay attention to their off-key, birdish rendition of *THE TORTOISE AND THE CHEETAH*.

When the group stopped to rest and Plush noticed Peter glancing around the trees nervously, he decided to break the silence.

"Hey, Peter, you have been quiet all day. I keep seeing you staring around the trees nervously. What's wrong?" said Plush.

Peter turned to face Plush and frowned. "I have a funny feeling," said Peter, shaking his head and thinking.

"I hope your funny feeling isn't hunger," said Plush laughing, though he immediately fell silent, realizing what "hungry" and "giant snake"--put together--meant.

"Maybe you are just tired or nervous. But, on the other hand, you haven't been in the wild for over a decade. So it's bound to make you feel a little off," said Plush.

But Peter shook his head and groaned, "You're probably right, Ape. It's just...look, I know it's crazy, but I don't think we have seen the last of those two humans," said Peter.

"What makes you say that?" said Plush curiously.

Peter shook his head. "I don't know, I just...have a feeling."

Plush was not sure how to respond. He scratched the back of his neck with his hand. His fingers passed over the collar the humans had put on him. Plush had almost forgotten about it. He had been so busy the last few days, focused on escaping and getting home. Plush was going to ask Peter if he knew how to get the collar off but decided not to. (Further discussion of humans was the last thing Peter needed). *"I'll just find a way to get this collar off when we get home,"* he thought.

As for Peter's fear that the two humans were still a danger to them, Plush shrugged it off and assumed Peter was just anxious...how very wrong he was.

After another hour of walking, Plush began to hear the sound of rushing water and knew they were getting close to the river. Percy flew ahead of the group and returned soon after with directions to the river. They reached the river bank within an hour.

The river was not very wide, maybe a hundred feet at most. The water was brown and murky, and the current was very strong. The river seemed alive; it roared louder than a large lion as thousands of gallons of water rushed through the narrow channel.

"Well, I've swum through worse," said Peter.

"I've swum through better," said Bongo, looking nervously at the brown, murky, rushing water.

"The current looks pretty strong, so it's best if we stay close to each other," said Peter.

"I will go first. Ape, you come next. Okay, Ape? APE?"

Peter looked around. Plush was standing twenty feet away from the river bank, looking scared.

"What's wrong? It's not as deep as it looks," said Peter.

"Uh," said Plush, looking embarrassed.

Peter waited for a response, and when none came, he shouted.

"SPIT IT OUT, APE!"

Plush sighed. "It's just, well... chimpanzees can't swim," he muttered.

"Really?" said Bongo. "I just thought apes were afraid of water."

Plush glared at Bongo. "Our legs are too short and don't bend the right way, and our bone structure is just too dense to float...."

"WE GET IT! YOU CAN'T SWIM, APE. NOW STOP WHIMPERING AND FIND AN ALTERNATIVE!" shouted Peter, clearly under a lot of stress.

"I might know a way," said Percy.

The small parrot had already flown across the river and back twice and waited patiently in the air. Peter, Plush, and Bongo looked at him.

"There is a human bridge a couple of miles upriver; maybe we could...."

"NOO!" yelled Peter and Plush at the same time.

"It's too dangerous," said Plush.

"You never mentioned a human bridge," said Peter hissing with anger. Percy cautiously rose a few extra feet in the air out of Peter's bite range.

"I *did* tell you there was a human way back to your savannah; there is a lonely mountain road humans use. They ride those creatures they call cars on it, but it is rarely traveled and very old. Anyway, it runs just past that mountain behind you." He pointed a wing to a massive mountain overlooking their valley. "There is a bridge a few miles upstream that crosses the river," Percy said, smiling innocently.

"YOU NEVER THOUGHT TO MENTION THAT FACT? FOR ALL WE KNOW, THOSE HUMANS WHO CAPTURED US COULD BE LESS THAN A MILE AWAY FROM US!" said Peter, looking more nervous than Plush had ever seen him.

"Peter, you have to calm down; panicking will get us nowhere," said Plush, though he, too, felt anxious.

Peter nodded, took a deep breath, and let out a loud HISS, which Plush assumed was the snake's way of taking a deep breath. Then the serpent looked around, and his eye widened.

"Hey, Ape, I know how you can cross the river," said Peter, and he pointed the tip of his massive tail at a large log lying on the river bank. "If you hold on to that, Bongo and I can push it along the river. It should float. Dead wood is usually lighter than ordinary wood."

Plush didn't have a better idea, so he and Bongo heaved the log into the river, and Plush wrapped his long arms around it. Bongo went to one end and Peter to another. Together, they dragged the log into the water and began to wade into the rushing current. It was much worse than Plush had thought. The current was so strong the log shifted unsteadily downstream.

Because Peter did not have hands and could only push the log along, much of the work went to Bongo, who was struggling so intensely that Plush feared at any moment the monkey would lose his grip and send them all rushing down the river to their deaths. Peter curled part of his body around the log, while the rest of him was in the water trying to propel the log forward with vigorous tail flapping. Percy was no help at all; the small parrot circled above the struggling group shouting out lousy advice over the roar of the raging river.

"YOU SHOULD MOVE TO THE LEFT A BIT. OK, NOW TURN TO THE RIGHT A BIT...WAIT...WHAT IS THAT? IT'S A CROCODILE! LOOK OUT! OH, NEVER MIND, IT'S JUST A ROCK! SORRY!"

"IF YOU WANT TO HELP, YOU CAN COME DOWN AND HELP US PUSH," said Peter.

"I AM A TWO-POUND BIRD; I DON'T THINK I WOULD BE MUCH HELP."

"THEN SHUT UP AND GO WAIT ON THE OTHER SIDE OF THE RIVER," roared Peter.

"BUT THAT WOULD BE BORING. YOU KNOW, THIS REMINDS ME OF THE TIME I SAW A HIPPO STUCK IN A MUD PIT. HE... AHHHHHHHH!!"

Percy squawked with horror and hurled himself through the air, narrowly missing the jaws of Peter, who had been so annoyed at the bird, he had lunged at him. It was a terrible mistake. Most of Peter's body flew up in the air, and then SLAM!

It was hard for any of them to remember exactly what happened next. Peter had gone flying into the air, causing the makeshift raft to shift violently as the full weight of the log was thrust onto Bongo. Then, with another loud SPLASH, Peter came crashing back onto the raft.

Poor Bongo did not have the strength to hold the raft in place by himself, and it careened dangerously down the river. Then, when 200 pounds of pure python slammed against the opposite end of the log, it was over.

Bongo screamed as the momentum sent him flying twelve feet into the air. He shouted, "AVENGE ME!" as he flew over Plush and smacked into Peter, causing the snake to tumble overboard. Peter and Bongo resurfaced long enough to hear Plush scream as the log raced uncontrollably down the rushing river.

Plush was terrified; the log was thrashing, spinning, and bouncing along as the dark, murky water pulled it down the river so fast the river bank was a blur of green and brown.

Plush closed his eyes. Waves slammed against the log; he felt it crash against rocks and other debris. The poor ape tried to plant his feet on the bottom of the river, but it was too deep, and even if he could, the current was too strong. Plush hung on, hugging the log as it sank underwater. He closed his eyes, waiting for death to come, but then the log came splashing back to the surface of the river. Before Plush could sigh with relief, the log twisted back under the waves, then SPLASH! It came crashing back to the surface. This happened again and again. Each time Plush was sure it would be his last.

Plush couldn't be sure just how long he was dragged down the river, but eventually, he heard someone shouting his name.

"PLUSH! PLUSH!" It was Percy. The small parrot flew over Plush, zooming around in the air.

For the first time in Plush's life, he was actually relieved to see the parrot.

"PERCY, DOWN HERE! HELP ME!" cried Plush, though he realized immediately something was wrong with Percy. The bird was shaking and shivering in the air. His eyes were full of fear--a fear not for himself but for Plush.

"BONGO AND PETER ARE NOT FAR BEHIND YOU-- ABOUT SIXTY METERS. THEY ALSO GOT STUCK IN THE CURRENT!" yelled Percy, his faint voice straining to be heard over the crashing rapids.

"YOU NEED TO GET OUT OF THE RIVER NOW, PLUSH!!" screamed Percy, panicked.

"THAT'S EASIER SAID THAN DONE. NOT ALL OF US CAN FLY, PERCY," said Plush, shouting to be heard over the rushing rapids and choking on a mouthful of muddy water.

"YOU DON'T UNDERSTAND, APE! YOU'RE ONLY A MILE AND A HALF AWAY FROM THE NAIROBI FALLS," said Percy.

"AM I SUPPOSED TO KNOW WHAT A NAIROBI FALL IS?" said Plush.

"THE NAIROBI FALLS IS THE HUMAN NAME FOR THE WATERFALL THAT THIS RIVER EMPTIES OVER. IT'S A 150 FOOT DROP ONTO A CLUSTER OF SHARP ROCKS. PLUSH, YOU'RE ONLY ABOUT A MILE AND A HALF AWAY FROM **CERTAIN DEATH!!!**"

CHAPTER 16
Persistent Humans

The sun was now in the center of the sky, its bright midday glare casting a golden light on the small bumpy road that curved around the mountain, going higher and higher. Big Ben and Little John sat in their Land Rover, too nervous to talk. They had been taking turns driving nonstop for over a day now, and, because their car was quite old and its air conditioner was not working properly, the two of them were sweating terribly. Little John had been passing the time by reading a book called **TO COOK A CHIMPANZEE** and playing Pac Man on his phone. He had been absent-mindedly humming to himself in the passenger seat when he looked up and noticed their location.

"BEN, what are you doing? This road leads to a dead end; we're supposed to be taking the mountain road down into the valley and across the river," said Little John.

Big Ben did not respond; instead, he pulled the Land Rover to a stop and stepped out of the car, looking ahead. Angry and tired, Little

John followed. As Little John had predicted, the road led to a dead end; the car was parked on a cliff edge overlooking a massive tropical rainforest. The view was stunning--miles and miles of dense jungle stretched across the horizon, and on either side of the valley, massive mountains stretched for miles in either direction. Far below, they could see a rushing river winding its way through the greenery like a giant python. The sight would have been breathtaking if they had not been under so much pressure.

"BEN, WHY ON EARTH DID YOU DRIVE US HERE? WE'RE SUPPOSED TO BE LOOKING FOR THAT APE," said Little John, fuming with anger. Big Ben glared at Little John and then rolled his eyes.

"JOHN, YOU IDIOT, I CAME UP HERE TO TRY TO GET CELL SIGNAL SO THE STUPID TRACKER WILL DO ITS JOB," roared Big Ben, looking angrier than ever. He took out his cell phone and, after staring at the screen, let out a roar of anger and hurled his brand new Iphone off the cliff's edge and down into the valley below.

"What is wrong? I thought you said the tracker on the ape would work even without a signal powered by GPS," said Little John, confused.

"It DOES work without cell signal, you moron, but the signal is much weaker. It will only show us the general location of the ape, not the *exact* location. Dr. Nile said that a phone signal would give us a more accurate location, but our blasted phones can't get an accurate location out in the middle of nowhere!" said Big Ben, furious.

"SO WHAT DO WE DO? We have to find that ape!"

Little John let out a loud moan of distress, took out his phone, and pulled up his tracker. There were no cell towers for miles so no there was no signal. The tracker showed that Plush was somewhere down in the valley. But there were miles of dense trees and animals down there.

Little John sighed. "Ben, it's hopeless; we're never going to find that ape on our own. We need more people and more equipment. We should head back and tell Mr. Winson. He will be upset, but maybe we could get off with minimal punishment. We are his cousins, after all."

Big Ben laughed, not out of humor, but out of fear and stress.

"John, do you really think Mr. Winson will be understanding just because we're his family? NO, OF COURSE NOT. WE ARE JUST EXPENDABLE PAWNS IN HIS PLAN. IF WE GO BACK EMPTY-HANDED, MR. WINSON WILL PROBABLY HAVE US CHOPPED INTO PIECES AND FED TO HIS DOGS AND THAT'S IF WE'RE LUCKY. MR. WINSON DOESN'T CARE THAT WE'RE FAMILY. HE HAS PROVEN HE CARES VERY LITTLE ABOUT THE PEOPLE WHO FAIL HIM, EVEN FAMILY. REMEMBER COUSIN JERRY?" Big Ben finished his rant and sat down defeated.

(And dear reader, no, I still don't know what happened to cousin Jerry, either.)

Big Ben stood up and began walking back to the car. Little John, however, had stopped; he looked down into the valley, squinting at something about a mile away floating in the river. He tried to make it out, but it was being pulled downstream very quickly. It might have been a log, but it seemed to be thrashing, almost as if it had limbs. Overrun by curiosity, Little John opened his backpack, pulled out a pair of binoculars, and began searching the river for the mysterious object.

Meanwhile, Big Ben opened the car door and climbed in; he felt sweat drip down the back of his neck, both from the heat and from his fear. Ben found himself thinking that he would probably die from heat stroke before he found the ape. However, his thoughts were broken by the sound of Little John shouting. Ben rushed out of the car. For one wild second, he thought Little John had fallen off the side of the cliff, but his fellow hunter was still sitting at the cliff's edge, his binoculars pressed hard against his face. Little John was shaking and shouting excitedly. Before Big Ben could ask what on earth was going on, Little John began screaming again.

"BEN! BEN! I SEE THE APE! LOOK! DOWN IN THE RIVER!! HE IS ON A LOG, AND, I DON'T BELIEVE IT!! BEN, LOOK! IT'S THE MONKEY AND THE SNAKE. THEY'RE ALSO IN THE RIVER!"

Without skipping a beat, Big Ben and Little John rushed to their car. They had a brief but fierce fight over who got to drive. Big Ben won, and Little John swore angrily at his larger companion and climbed into the passenger seat. Big Ben did a 360 degree turn and slammed on the gas pedal.

Ten minutes later the car was speeding down the mountain, zooming over narrow twisty roads dangerously close to the edge. When they reached its base, Big Ben swerved the car off the main road and went off-roading into the jungle. He accelerated, crushing the dense undergrowth in his path and speeding towards the river. With the road behind them, their minds focused on only one thing: getting that ape.

CHAPTER 17
Lucky Bongo

The current was picking up. Plush could feel it. Plush had no idea how long he had been in the river, but he could tell it was midday because the sun burned brightly overhead. The river looped and turned, curling around bends and trapping the poor ape in the center of the river. He knew he was getting closer to the falls. Behind him, he sensed, rather than heard, Peter and Bongo being pulled along the river. "And they said they were good swimmers," scoffed Plush.

There was nothing he could do. He could not swim, and he couldn't control the log, but the idea of letting go of it was equally terrifying, so he hung on as the river pulled him closer and closer to death.

Behind him, he faintly heard Bongo and Peter screaming and hollering as they were also helplessly trapped in the river's clutches.

"YOU SAID YOU'VE SWAM THROUGH WORSE," screamed Bongo.

"I HAVE, BUT IT HAS BEEN A WHILE. I SPENT THE LAST 12 YEARS LOCKED UP IN A CAGE." SPLASH! "I AM A LITTLE RUSTY, IF YOU DIDN'T KNOW," hissed Peter.

The monkey was hanging on to the end of Peter's tail; his arms, legs, and tail were hugging the massive snake. Peter was equally terrified, and Bongo's screaming was not helping. Peter tried to swim with the current in an attempt to catch up to Plush; however, the river was too rough and strong.

Percy was flying through the air above the snake and monkey, trying to think of a way to save them. As he pondered their dire situation, he was distracted by something out of the corner of his eye. Moving through the dense trees on the west side of the river bank (the same one they had started on) something very big and very fast was zooming through the trees, bouncing along and coming closer and closer to the river bank. After realizing what it was, he had just enough time to yell, "LOOK OUT!" before the thing burst out of the trees and came into full view of Peter and Bongo.

It was a car, a large 1993 neon-blue Land Rover, and sitting inside it were the sneering faces of none other than Big Ben and Little John.

Bongo let out a high-pitched shriek. "OH NO, IT'S THOSE GUYS! HOW DID THEY FIND US?"

Peter was frozen with terror, unable to fight the rushing water anymore; he just stopped moving and let himself be dragged downstream. The humans and their car were now speeding along the river bank beside them, but they were not paying any attention to the snake and monkey. The car raced ahead, turned a bend on the river bank, and was out of sight.

It only took Peter a moment to realize why they had been completely ignored.

"PERCY, THEY'RE GOING AFTER PLUSH! YOU NEED TO GO WARN HIM!" Peter looked around; Percy was already flying ahead, panic in the small bird's eyes.

"WHAT ARE WE GOING TO DO? WE HAVE TO HELP PLUSH," said Peter more to himself than to Bongo, who was now shaking his head, screaming, "IT'S JUST A DREAM, IT'S JUST A DREAM, IT'S JUST A...."

"IT'S JUST A COUPLE OF ARMED HUMANS WHO WANT TO KILL US!" yelled Peter, and as he yelled, he got an idea.

Without warning, Peter plunged underwater, dragging poor Bongo behind him. Bongo didn't even have time to scream before the air was sucked out of his lungs and replaced with muddy water. Then Peter shot out of the river and spun high up into the air. Using all of his strength, he sent Bongo flying off his back and towards the river bank. Bongo crashed into a tree and hit the ground unharmed (although he was still screaming ten seconds after he had landed). Finally, he got up and began jogging along the riverbank, trying to keep up with Peter.

At first, Bongo thought Peter had thrown him to safety, but then he realized which side of the river he was on.

"HEY, PETER, YOU THREW ME ON THE WRONG SIDE OF THE RIVER! HOME IS THAT WAY," he pointed angrily at the other side of the river.

Peter ignored the monkey's comments and shouted back, drowning out Bongo's protests. "BONGO, LISTEN! YOU ARE THE ONLY ONE WHO CAN SAVE PLUSH. GO AND ATTACK THE HUMANS' CAR-CREATURE! ATTACK ITS ROLLING LEGS, STAB THEM WITH A ROCK OR SOMETHING. IT SHOULD SLOW THEIR STEED DOWN. HURRY, I WILL TRY TO GET TO PLUSH BEFORE HE REACHES THE FALLS."

Meanwhile, Plush was utterly unaware of the humans; he was still hanging onto the log, being pulled faster and faster down the river. Every time the river curved around a bend, he strained to see the massive waterfalls, but he hadn't reached them yet. Nonetheless, his fear kept growing and growing; it seemed like the river was providing the most depressing and maddening death possible.

"Can this day get ANY WORSE?" he thought.

Apparently, it could. As if in answer to his question, Percy, the parrot, came flying around a corner, shouting so loudly it was almost inaudible. Plush understood only one word: HUMANS.

The Land Rover came speeding around the corner with its powerful headlights on (even though it was midday and sunny). Its horn was blaring as the car zoomed up the river bank and accelerated to match Plush's speed.

The car was right-hand drive, and the passenger window facing Plush was rolled down. Little John, who was laughing hysterically, stuck half his body out of the window holding a massive something that closely resembled a bazooka. He pointed it at Plush and pulled the trigger.

There was a gigantic WOOSH, and a tangle of wires shot out of it and sailed through the air towards Plush who had ducked behind the log. The ape heard the mass of string and wires slam against the log; he peeked over the edge of the log and saw that the mass of wires formed a net and that the thing Little John had fired at him was a net gun. Little John laughed and reloaded his net gun and fired again.

Big Ben and Little John were having the time of their lives; they had been so worried about Plush eluding them, and now that they were so close, the two humans were toying with Plush, getting revenge for all the trouble the ape had caused them.

If you could see the scene from above, you would be able to see just how absurd it all was: an ape hurtling uncontrollably down a river clutching a log while two grown men bounced along on the river bank firing nets at him. Behind them, a drenched monkey was running after the car, bellowing and waving his arms in the air, trying to get the car's attention. And bringing up the rear, a massive snake was being pounded by wave after wave of muddy water as he was spun and tossed through the rolling rapids.

"HEY JOHN, SAVE THE LAST NET. WE WILL NEED IT FOR THE MONKEY," said Big Ben shouting to be heard over the river's roar and the car engine's groaning. He grabbed the net gun out of Little John's hands and handed him a tranquilizer gun instead. "AND, JOHN, TRY TO ACTUALLY HIT THE APE. THE SOONER WE CAN GET BACK TO NAIROBI, THE SOONER WE CAN MAKE THAT APE SOMEBODY ELSE'S PROBLEM."

The idea of finally getting rid of Plush was exhilarating for both of them.

Little John took aim and fired.

Plush felt the dart slip past him less than an inch away from his left ear. He couldn't believe it! He was sure the humans wanted him alive, but now they were shooting sleeping darts at him. Didn't they realize he was less than a mile away from falling 150 feet onto sharp rocks? And if he were sedated when he fell, his death would be guaranteed.

Didn't these humans know about the falls? But then a thought occurred to Plush: what if the humans didn't know about the falls? It made sense that they were trying to sedate Plush to capture him, but it seemed like they had no idea the falls even existed; this made them an even bigger threat.

Plush was getting tired. He had been able to dodge all of the tranquilizers simply because he would spin the log around every time one was fired. Still, it was exhausting, and he knew he couldn't hold out much longer.

A final dart flew towards Plush, and he knew there was no stopping it; his arms were too tired to shift the log out of the way. He closed his eyes, waiting for the dart to make an impact, but suddenly, the log lurched sideways so quickly and unexpectedly that Plush lost his grip and felt it slip out from under him.

Suddenly, he felt a scaly tail encircle him, pulling him to the surface. "I TOLD YOU I'VE SWUM THROUGH WORSE, APE," said a familiar voice.

Plush couldn't believe it. "PETER! BUT HOW DID YOU...? WHERE IS BONGO?"

"LATER! WE NEED TO GET OUT OF THE RIVER NOW," yelled Peter. Unfortunately, it was too late. As they rounded a final corner, the waterfall came into view.

It looked like the world just ended as the water poured over the falls causing massive blankets of fog to cover the surrounding area.

"NOO!!" yelled Plush, and he tried in vain to paddle the log-raft to shore, but it was no use. Knowing there was nothing he could do, Plush simply closed his eyes and clung onto the log as he and Peter disappeared over the edge.

Big Ben had seen the falls but he didn't realize just how big they were. However, he noticed that the land next to the falls sloped down very steeply, and he slammed his foot on the brakes. The car slid a bit on the uneven muddy ground and was feet away from falling over the edge.

SLASH!

The two humans heard the sound of ripping rubber coming from behind them, and they both turned around just in time to see something *WOOSH* past the window.

Bongo was swinging on a vine. He flew over the Land Rover and went hurtling through the air. He shouted "CANNONBALL!!" and stuck his tongue out at the humans, but then he realized there was nothing but air underneath him, and he screamed as he went sailing right over the falls' edge.

Big Ben and Little John were left speechless; however, a sudden shift in their vehicle brought them back to their senses. The back left tire of their car had been completely ripped to shreds by Bongo. Unfortunately, the uneven, muddy ground underneath them caused the car to slide a few feet forward, and as Little John climbed back through the car window, the vehicle seemed to totter on the edge of the steep slope, and then it *fell.*

Big Ben and Little John screamed as the car tumbleed down the mountainside, rolling and spinning down the massive slope. There were a series of bangs as the car's airbags burst to life. And still, the car fell, crashing against rocks and plants. It smashed against trees that were growing vertically off the cliff's edge.

After what seemed like the eternity of hell, the car finally came to a stop. The two men were no longer screaming; all was silent. The Land Rover was a wreck. What had once been an expensive antique vehicle was now a pile of broken metal lying upside down in a deep ditch. All the windows were smashed, and the roof had partially caved in. Smoke was rising from where the engine had been, and pieces of the car were scattered all around the ditch.

Through a small hole in the smashed roof, a dark red liquid was trickling onto the ground, and the small parrot who cautiously peeked out from behind a nearby tree knew immediately that it was blood. Percy gave a shout of relief, flew high into the air, and took off, flying away to locate his friends. If he had stayed a moment longer, he would have seen the hand--a bloodstained, partially dislocated hand, rise slowly out of the smashed window. After feeling around the ground, it retreated as its owner pulled it back into the wrecked car...

CHAPTER 18
Percy's Secret Mission

Plush was sure he was dead. The last thing he remembered was falling over the waterfall, hearing it roar, and then nothing. The dark void he was lying in seemed so calm and peaceful, completely different from anything he had experienced in his past life.

He lay there for a long time without a care in the world before he became aware of something; he was still breathing. This was puzzling: did dead apes breathe? And if he was dead, why was his heart still beating? That proved he must still be alive. With a great effort, Plush opened his eyes. The sun was setting over the distant mountains, and Plush realized he must have been out for several hours at least. He looked around. He was lying on a river bank, and he was pleased and confused to see that he was on the opposite bank from the one they had started on. To his amazement, he could no longer hear the rushing waterfall. That meant he must be miles away from the falls, but how on earth did he travel that far if he was unconscious? Even more impressive was how he had survived the fall and emerged relatively unharmed. (Well, except for the massive bump on his head.)

"So the Ape lives, once again," said a voice.

Plush jumped up and spun around. Peter the Python was lying in the grass behind him. Plush felt overjoyed, and without thinking, he ran forward and hugged the massive snake. Peter looked surprised and immediately shrugged Plush off him.

"Good to see you, Ape," he said.

"But the waterfall, the rocks, the humans, what happened?" asked Plush, sputtering.

Peter sighed. "Apparently, this area has been getting a lot of rain recently which caused the river to rise. It rose high enough to flow over the rocks, and even though we fell over the falls, the rocks were deep enough not to be a serious danger. Since you were out cold, Bongo and I dragged you down the river for a few miles until the river calmed down, and we were able to get to shore."

"Where is Bongo?" said Plush, realizing that the monkey was nowhere to be found. Peter frowned, looking annoyed.

"Bongo and Percy thought you were dead. Yeah, they are digging a grave for you," said Peter blankly. Plush wasn't sure whether to feel amused, honored, or alarmed at the fact his friends were taking the time to dig him a grave when he wasn't even dead.

At that exact moment, Bongo and Percy emerged from the woods, Bongo caught sight of Plush, and screamed. Plush covered his ears as a high-pitched shriek filled the air.

"AHHHH!!!! GHOST APE!!!" yelled Bongo, and he leapt back, tripped over his tail, and landed on top of poor Percy, who had been hovering behind him.

Plush rolled his eyes.

"Bongo, I am not dead," said Plush.

Bongo, however, was not convinced and shrieked. "AHHH, IT'S A LYING GHOST APE!!"

It took a while to convince Bongo that Plush was indeed NOT dead, but once they did, he calmed down enough to tell Plush everything, especially what had happened with the humans. Percy was happy to explain Big Ben and Little John's supposed fate.

"Well, Bongo stabbed the car's tire thing, and it stumbled or something, and fell down the cliff, and when it came to a stop, it was in pieces; no way it survived," said Percy looking relieved.

"And the humans, what happened to them?" said Plush, eagerly awaiting the answer.

"The car was lying upside down, and the humans were crushed underneath it," said Percy.

Plush felt relief wash over him. He looked at Peter. Clearly, the snake was also stunned.

"Oh, and there is more good news. We made great time today, and if you guys keep this pace up, you might just make it back to your forest before the baboons destroy your tribe, Plush, and the northern apes destroy your tribe, Bongo."

Three days had passed since they escaped the human city and three days were still left to make it home before the baboons attacked the ape forest. After a short rest, they continued their journey. As they walked, Percy sat on Plush's shoulder, happily recalling his many travels.

"You have been everywhere," said Plush, amazed as Percy recounted his many adventures.

"Yeah, flying has its benefits. I have traveled all over the continent," said Percy.

"Man, your life is so awesome, so free," said Plush.

"It's all thanks to my wings. I don't know who I would be if I couldn't fly," said Percy as he eagerly recounted a story about the time he flew all the way to Cairo, Egypt, and got to see the Great Pyramids. (Though in reality, he had no idea what Egypt, Cairo, or pyramids really were; all he could describe were massive "triangle mountains.")

Percy was clearly enjoying the spotlight, and Plush couldn't help but feel jealous of him. The parrot didn't seem to have a single problem; he could do whatever he wanted whenever he wanted; he didn't have responsibilities or rules in his life. Plush also realized that, unlike the rest of the group, Percy was willingly helping them; he didn't have to. He didn't have to help them escape, and he did not have a tribe in danger of being wiped out as he and Bongo did.

"You know, I could probably fly all the way to your savanna and back in less than two days," said Percy smugly. Plush was slightly taken aback at this new information. And an idea slowly formed in the ape's head.

"So, you're telling me you could fly all the way to...I don't know...MY forest and back in less than two days? Then why are you still here with us?" said Plush, confused.

"Well, I like being with Bongo, and it seems like you guys REALLY need my help," said Percy half-heartedly.

"I have one more question, Percy," said Plush, making sure he was out of earshot of the others before he continued.

"Sure, what is it?" said Percy. Plush nervously made quite sure the others wouldn't hear him before he continued.

"Percy," said Plush, "Could you deliver a message for me? Please, it's really important, and if for some reason I don't make it home in time, I will never forgive myself."

"Look, Plush, I would love to, but don't you guys need me to help you navigate back to your savannah?" said Percy.

"Well," said Plush, choosing his next words very carefully. "What if you give me directions back to our savannah, and you could fly, deliver the message, and be back here in two days tops?" said Plush, praying the parrot would oblige his request.

Percy was slightly taken aback. One part of him wanted to refuse the request, claiming he was needed here, but looking into the ape's eyes, he could see the desperation and pleading in them. And Percy, despite being a nosy and annoying bird, was not a cruel one. He glanced curiously at Plush. Percy looked right into Plush's eyes and tilted his head curiously. "What kind of message?"

Several hours later, the four animals set up camp in a small clearing. The sun was setting, and Bongo, Plush, and Percy munched away on nuts and fruit. Peter had located the body of a recently deceased gazelle and was enjoying his first real meal in over a decade.

As Percy and Bongo sang songs in excruciatingly agonizing voices, Plush sat next to Peter who seemed happier than Plush had ever seen him before; he was laughing and joking with Bongo and Percy and even joined in some of their singing (which just made it more unbearable for Plush to listen to). Plush was sure he knew what the source of Peter's new found joy was.

"It must feel great, you know, knowing the humans are out of our lives forever," said Plush.

Peter nodded. "It just feels like a dream. I dreamed about escaping that horrible place for years, and now that I actually did, I can't believe it!" he smiled and took another bite of the gazelle.

Plush, however, was not as cheerful as the others. He remembered when Peter had told him about his fear that the humans were following them, and now Plush was equally anxious about another mystery. How on earth had humans found them? It didn't make any sense that the humans, even in their car, would have never been able to catch up to the group unless they already knew exactly where they were. And that was impossible, right?

Plush sat thinking, rolling the day's events over in his mind and finally coming to a conclusion: even if the humans had somehow magically known their location, it didn't matter anymore; they were dead. And with that comforting thought in mind, he drifted off to sleep.

Unfortunately for Plush, it wouldn't be the last time he underestimated humans.

CHAPTER 19
Broken Humans

By the time Big Ben regained consciousness, he had been stuck in the wrecked car for over three hours. The PAIN was the first thing he felt even before he was fully awake. His body was searing with pain. Each of his limbs had multiple cuts, scrapes, and bruises. His hand felt partially dislocated. He was bleeding everywhere. However, the car's seat belts, airbags, and roll cage had done their job. He was alive, and due to the loud moaning next to him, he was pretty sure Little John had survived the crash as well. When he opened his eyes, he also became aware that the world was upside down. NO, he was upside down. His seat belt had locked and kept him hanging, unconscious, upside down. Had the car been a decade older they wouldn't have survived. Had the car been a decade newer, their injuries would be far less severe.

The car was lying in a ditch next to the falls, and the waterfall's roar was so loud Big Ben could barely hear his own panicked breathing. Little John was also banged up-- worse than Big Ben since he had not had time to put his seatbelt back on properly before the car plummeted. He had been bounced around the car's interior for the duration of the fall. His nose was broken, and he had a massive piece of glass stuck in the flesh of his left thigh.

"What happened?" said Little John, who had freed himself and was trying to climb out of the smashed car window.

Big Ben did not respond; he was attempting to heave himself through his partially caved-in window, trying to ignore the pain from his many wounds.

Neither of them remembered much from the crash. They had both taken massive hits to the head, and their memory of the impact was a bit foggy.

It took over an hour for both of them to crawl out of the car, and once they had escaped the wreckage, they collapsed on the ground, panting and gasping, too weak to move or even speak.

There is a breaking point for everybody; all humans have one. They reach the point where they lose all hope, when they simply accept their fate and freeze. They don't care about anything anymore; they just collapse and, at times, won't even lift a finger to save their own lives. This often occurs after a traumatic experience, primarily in remote areas where there is little to no hope of rescue. When this happens, the human mind undergoes such physical and psychological torment that the brain just blocks all emotion. The traumatized or wounded just lay there with no fight left in them and no will to survive. Big Ben and Little John were perfect examples of this.

They lay in the grass, their breathing slowing down as the will to do anything drained from their bodies. It had started to rain, and although heavy drops fell on the pair of them, still, they didn't move. They didn't even bother trying to crawl to the shade of a tree; they just lay there as their blood-soaked clothes were filled with water.

As gallons of water drops fell on their exposed and cut skin, the blood was washed away and the ground around them slowly turned to mud. If Big Ben and Little John's minds had been working properly, they would have found the rain unbearable and annoying, however in this state, they felt nothing at all, not even pain. Neither of them knew just how long they lay there. The clouds in the sky were so dark it might have been the middle of the day or the middle of the night-- not like they cared.

However, after a while, Big Ben became aware that the pain from his banged-up body had slightly lessened. The cuts had stopped bleeding, and the blood hardened on his exposed skin. Slowly, his mind began to recover from the traumatic breakdown, and Big Ben's mind began to regain control of his body. Unbeknownst to him, the same thing was happening to Little John; they were both starting to regain control of their traumatized brains just as the rain began to die down and bright sunlight began to shine through the clouds.

Then slowly, painfully, the two humans pushed themselves to upright positions as they felt the adrenaline and anger return to their bodies. They were both still exhausted, but determination now fueled them.

"John, get the first aid kit. It should be in the trunk," groaned Big Ben. Little John nodded and crawled around the wreck to the smashed remains of the vehicle's trunk. Ben joined him, and together, as they removed the smashed trunk door from the rest of the car, a depressing sight met their eyes.

"Noo!!" moaned Little John miserably.

Everything in the trunk had either been destroyed in the fall or soaked by the torrential rain.

"Oh great," said Big Ben, "All our water is gone," he moaned, pointing at a dozen smashed plastic bottles.

Their portable GPS and their satellite phone had also been soaked and were no longer working; the only food they could find was a drenched box of protein bars.

"GREAT, ALL OUR FOOD, ALL OUR WATER, AND ALL OUR DEVICES ARE RUINED!" yelled Big Ben, and in his anger, he kicked one of the upside-down tires, though it only bruised his leg even more.

"WELL, WHAT'S NOT RUINED?" said Little John rolling his eyes.

In truth, not much; most of their belongings had been destroyed in the fall, and even the items that survived the fall were now drenched and unusable. All they could recover was a sawed-off shotgun (and nine shotgun rounds), a bow (and six arrows), a first aid kit, several rain-soaked maps they found in the glove compartment, a single hunting knife, and a compass.

Ben looked through the maps; he swore loudly upon realizing that the maps were written in Swahili, not English. Since he could barely speak Swahili, much less read it, he could not understand any of the words written on it. Nevertheless, he did his best to find their location. Even though the map was in Swahili, it had a clearly-drawn picture of the falls in the southeast corner. Bingo! Now he could use the compass to navigate. All was not lost.

"Ok, if that's the falls, then we're somewhere around here." He pointed to a small spot on the map.

Little John glared at his companion, annoyed that he was so optimistic.

"Well, now that you're finished using a map, you can't even read, WHAT ARE WE GOING TO DO? WE LOST THE APE, THE SNAKE, AND THE MONKEY. WE'RE DONE FOR! MR. WINSON WILL HAVE OUR HEADS--AND THAT'S IF

WE'RE LUCKY ENOUGH EVEN TO FIND A WAY OUT OF THIS PROLONGED PURGATORY!"

Big Ben stood up and turned to face his colleague.

"LOOK. WE CAN REPLACE THE BABOON AND THE PYTHON--IT WON'T BE HARD TO FIND SUBSITES FOR THOSE TWO--BUT MR. WINSON WANTS ONE OF THE WHITE-HAIRED CHIMPS, AND THOSE ARE AS RARE AS A NORTHERN WHITE RHINO. WE CAN AFFORD TO LOSE THE SNAKE AND MONKEY. MR. WINSON HAS EYES ONLY FOR THAT APE."

"EXACTLY MY POINT!" said Little John.

He was about to respond when he paused and slowly reached a hand into his pocket and pulled out his phone.

In all the chaos of the last day, Little John had completely forgotten that he still had a phone. However, the phone had also taken a toll in the crash; its screen was cracked, and bits of glass were missing from the frame. Crossing his fingers, he pressed the home button and...

"NO WAY, BEN, COME HERE! MY PHONE! IT STILL WORKS! WE CAN STILL USE THE TRACKER!" said Little John jumping with excitement, though he immediately regretted it as his injured leg was not ready for that.

Big Ben's eyes widened at the sight.

"That's Great, John, but we can't follow it just yet," said Big Ben.

"WHY NOT," said Little John glaring angrily at his companion.

"WELL, THINK ABOUT IT," roared Big Ben. "FIRSTLY, WERE STUCK IN THE MIDDLE OF NOWHERE WITH BARELY ANY SUPPLIES. SECONDLY, LOOK AT US!

WE'RE BOTH BADLY INJURED AND PROBABLY NEED TO GET TO A HOSPITAL AS SOON AS POSSIBLE. FACE IT, JOHN, WE'RE IN NO CONDITION TO GO APE HUNTING.THIRDLY, THAT STUPID TRACKER IS NOT VERY PRECISE WITHOUT CELL SIGNAL. WE CAN'T NARROW DOWN THE APE'S PRECISE LOCATION!" Big Ben finished his rant, his throat sore from all the yelling.

"WELL, IF YOU'RE SO SMART, WHAT DO YOU THINK WE SHOULD DO?" said Little John, challenging him.

"Find the nearest village or town. Get to a hospital. After we are discharged, we go back to the warehouse to grab more supplies--better supplies. After that,we can track down the ape and capture him, and Mr. Winson never has to know it got away," finished Ben.

Little John grunted in agreement; it was their best option.

Big Ben returned to his maps and did his best to locate the nearest human settlement.

"Well, John, It looks like the nearest town is Ng'ombe Miji or whatever it's called. It's the same place we found that ape."

Little John looked annoyed. "Are you sure it's the closest? How far is the next closest town?"

"Well, there is a small city, but it's 200 kilometers back the way we came; that cow village where we found the ape is less than half that, only about 80 kilometers from here, give or take a few."

Little John glanced over Big Ben's shoulder and back at his phone. His eyes widened like a child opening a birthday present. "BLOODY HELL, BEN! LOOK!" said Little John shoving his phone into Big Ben's face.

"BEN, YOU NEED TO SEE THIS!!! IF THE TRACKER'S LOCATION IS CORRECT, THEN IT LOOKS LIKE THE

APE IS HEADING BACK EAST WHERE WE FIRST FOUND IT."

Big Ben looked from the tracker and back to the map many times; he felt adrenaline and a rush of excitement. A mix of eagerness and common sense gripped him. Finally, he came to a decision.

"All right, John, listen, we're going to follow that ape, but only as long as it heads in the general direction of its savannah; if it veers off course at any time and starts traveling away from the savannah, we forget it and keep going towards the village. If we catch up to it before it reaches the savanna, we'll kill its companions and take the ape alive. DEAL?" said Big Ben.

He reached out a hand to Little John, and Little John thought for a second, then shook Big Ben's hand and said,

"DEAL."

Big Ben grabbed the sawed-off shotgun, and Little John took his bow and arrows, and together, the two humans began the long trek back to civilization...

CHAPTER 20
Plush's Secret

When Percy and Bongo woke up from their night's rest, the first thing they noticed was that Percy was nowhere to be found. Plush was already awake, and when Peter asked him of Percy's whereabouts, he was vague in detail.

"Oh, Percy is just running an errand for me," said Plush, and he tried to shift the subject. "Before he left, he told me that all we need to do is follow the river east until it splits into two runoffs. We turn south, and it's a brief hike over some rocky mountains, then we are back in the savanna," continued Plush, who eagerly began to jog along the river bank.

As the day wore on, Percy's absence started making Peter and Bongo slightly nervous; Plush, however, remained cheerful and energetic. Peter tried asking Plush where he had sent Percy, but Plush never gave a reasonable answer. Instead, he simply said that Percy would be back soon and not to worry.

Of course, this made Bongo panic, and he started trying to guess Percy's whereabouts, even going as far as accusing Plush and Peter of eating him.

The interrogation only got worse as the day progressed.

The three animals followed the river, and when it split, they left the river and started moving south. They realized how dangerous it was to leave the only water source they knew of in an area they had no experience with. Around midday, the terrain became steeper and rockier. The trees started to thin out and eventually became faint and few. An amazing view stretched below them. The trees stretched out over a valley of breathtaking beauty. The mountains in the distance were blue and cloudy, and if Plush squinted hard and focused on the distant horizon, he could make out the tiny silhouettes of dozens of tall buildings: the city where they had started from. The sight was very humbling for the animals. Although they had come far, it was not far enough. If they could still see the human towers, they needed to escape the human lands, and as long as there were skyscrapers on the horizon, they had not truly escaped; they were not free not until no sight of the terrible human lands could be seen.

The rocky hills slowed the group significantly. Even Plush and Bongo, both natural climbers, did not fare well in these conditions. Plush was a tree climber, not a mountain climber, and Bongo, a Chacma Baboon, mainly lived on flat grasslands. Peter, of course, was just a snake and was naturally slow.

Unfortunately and unknown to Plush and his friends, the rocky uneven terrain favored the tall bipedal legs and bodies of humans who were better suited for this environment. Even injured, Big Ben and Little John made great time, dangerously closing the gap between them and their unsuspecting quarry.

"I wish I was a mountain gorilla," said Plush, panting as they clambered over boulders and rocks.

Plush, Bongo, and Peter were all exhausted and dangerously--and peacefully--unaware of the terrible threat that was pursuing them...

"OK, PLUSH, THAT'S IT. I HAVE LOST MY PATIENCE WITH YOU. TELL US WHAT YOU DID WITH PERCY!" roared Peter, who was angry, not because Percy was absent, but because of a lack of information from Plush. Snakes hate being left in the dark.

(That, my reader, was just an ironic metaphor. Snakes, as you know, love the dark.)

Plush didn't know why he wanted to keep the Percy mission secret from the others--probably because he was sure they would disapprove. In the end, though, he knew it was impossible to keep the mission undercover.. After all, Percy would surely blab. That bird couldn't keep a secret if his life depended on it.

✱✱✱

It was the evening of the fourth day since Plush, Peter, and Bongo had escaped from the human city.

Percy was soaring over the hills, his wings flapping like a high-powered fan. As he sped over the savannah grasslands, his eyes were so focused on the ground that he was not looking where he was flying and crashed into a flock of fellow parrots, causing them to break formation and scatter. He caught himself before hitting the ground and kept flying, shouting hurried apologies behind him.

"SORRY, PHIL! SORRY, BILL! SORRY, MOM!" he shouted. And he kept flying.

In the distance, he could see the ape forest, a patch of green against the tan savannah grass. He was nearing the coast and could hear the waves and smell the saltwater.

As he reached his destination, he descended through the trees. The chimpanzees were panicking; some were running around gathering weapons, and some were screaming and crying for loved ones. He scanned the forest floor and spotted a group of apes standing in a clearing arguing, and the parrot flew, undetected, into a dense tree where he perched himself on a branch. Percy descended a few feet so he could hear the conversation.

"TRAVIS, WE HAVE ALL THE APES WHO ARE ABLE TO CARRY A SPEAR READY TO FIGHT, BUT WE JUST DON'T HAVE ENOUGH CHIMPS TO HOLD OFF THAT MANY MONKEYS," said a panicked council member.

Travis, however, seemed too angry to feel scared.

"WELL, WHAT OTHER CHOICE DO WE HAVE? THEY STILL THINK WE KIDNAPPED BRUNO'S STUPID SON, AND NOTHING WE DO WILL CHANGE THEIR MINDS. WE CAN'T RUN. THEY ARE FASTER AND WOULD TRACK US DOWN AND SLAUGHTER US. WE CAN'T HIDE. THEY KNOW THIS SAVANNAH JUST AS WELL, IF NOT BETTER THAN WE DO."

Percy was so focused on the conversation he didn't notice the long, black, fur-covered arm slinking up behind him.

"WE NEED TO THINK OF SOMETHING!" yelled Mucha angrily.

Suddenly, Percy felt something lunge at him from behind and seize his small body. They were hands. Large, furry, strong hands clamped around his chest so fast the poor bird barely had time to squawk in surprise.

Brandon, the headhunter chimpanzee, leapt out of a low hanging tree and backflipped into the clearing with poor Percy clutched in his hands.

"Hey, Travis, look! This bird was spying on us!" said Brandon, holding out Percy. The ape council closed in around Percy, curious and somewhat hungry. Percy was horrified. Apart from Plush, he had never been in close proximity to an ape before. When Plush had told him that he was a runt chimp, Percy assumed he was just slightly smaller in size than his relatives, however, the apes closing in around him were nothing like Plush. It was hard to believe they were even the same species. These chimps were big--much bigger than Plush. Their faces were twisted and scarred, their teeth were crooked and chipped, their eyes were darker and more primal than Plush's. The poor parrot was shaking with fear, sure that these hideous faces would be the last he ever saw.

Travis looked down at the small bird in Brandon's arms and watched it shake and twitch with fear.

"WHO ARE YOU, WHAT IS YOUR NAME, AND WHAT ARE YOU DOING HERE? YOU'RE NOT ONE OFF OUR MESSENGERS BIRDS. THEY FLED UP NORTH AFTER NEWS OF THE BABOON-PLANNED ATTACK. WHY WERE YOU SPYING ON US?" bellowed Travis, his powerful, deep voice echoing throughout the forest.

Percy lifted his small head and spoke in a squeaky, soft voice. "My name is Percy Patrick Parrotbird, the Third," squeaked Percy. "I have a message for an ape named Purcellville. His grandson, Plush, sent me." Percy's voice was growing fainter from fear, and he was barely able to squeak.

Travis glanced at the ape council looking confused. Then, he looked at his fellow chimps and burst out laughing. The other chimps joined in, their loud beastly voices echoed across the savannah. Finally, Travis stopped laughing and his voice returned to its original tone. "NICE TRY, BIRD," said Travis, and his burn-marked face twisted from laughter to anger. "PLUSH IS DEAD. HE WAS KILLED BY HUMANS TWO WEEKS AGO, AND HIS GRANDFATHER, PURCELLVILLE, IS LIKELY GOING THE SAME DIRECTION. NOW TELL US THE TRUTH OR WE'RE HAVING PARROT PASTA FOR DINNER. YOU TALK OR YOU DIE!"

So Percy talked. He talked about Plush being kidnapped and how he had found Bongo and Peter and teamed up with them to escape from the humans. He explained everything and concluded with Plush asking him to send a message to his grandfather.

When he finished, the ape council was silent, and for a brief second, Percy thought they might believe his story, but then they burst out laughing AGAIN.

This time they laughed for a lot longer, and Percy knew there was no getting through to these apes. He had hoped that Brandon might lessen his hold on him due to laughing so hard, but no. Percy remained trapped in the chimpanzee's hands.

"THAT WAS THE STUPIDEST, FUNNIEST STORY I EVER HEARD. ESCAPING A HUMAN CITY! AND JUST 'HAPPENING' TO FIND BRUNO'S MISSING SON!" The apes laughed and laughed until finally they steadied themselves.

"BECAUSE YOU AMUSED ME, YOU PATHETIC PIGEON, WE WILL LET YOU LIVE, BUT BE WARNED: IF YOU EVER COME BACK TO THIS PLACE SPREADING RIDICULOUS RUMORS AND OUTLANDISH STORIES, WE SHALL FEAST ON YOUR FEATHERS," and laughing like the mad ape he was, Travis yanked Percy out of Brandon's hands and threw the poor parrot thirty feet in the air.

As his trembling subsided, Percy sighed in defeat. He would have to fly back to Plush, Bongo, and Peter and tell them the bad news.

Percy's heart pounded with adrenaline as he flew high into the air. He flew to the top of a dense tree out of sight of the apes on the ground. Sheer terror and Brandon's vice grip had caused him to lose his breath! He rested on a branch, his heart pounding in his chest; he was too out of breath to fly just yet.

Suddenly, for the second time that day, he felt a strong furry hand seize him so quickly his brain barely had time to panic.

"NO! PLEASE DON'T TURN ME INTO A PARROT PASTA!! I WON'T TASTE GOOD," he cried, but a hand covered his beak before he could let out another cry. The hands turned him around, and he saw the ape holding him. Strangely enough, he felt slightly less scared this time.

The ape holding him was smaller than Travis and all the council members. Its face was much less beastly than the other apes'. Its teeth were much straighter, and its eyes were different then the other apes'. They looked very similar to Plush's. The ape looked around making sure he was out of earshot of the rest of his tribe. Then he whispered to Percy, "Be quiet. I am not going to hurt you," and he slowly let go of Percy.

165

Part of Percy's mind was screaming *STRANGER DANGER! FLY AWAY!* But another part of him kept him rooted to the spot. Somehow he knew this ape ment him no harm.

"Who are you?" said Percy curiously.

"I am Albert Apeinstein," said the ape, looking around and clearly wanting to keep quiet. "I heard you talking to Travis. You said Plush sent you, and you had a message for Purcellville. Is that true?"

Percy was still trying to recover from his panic attack and could only muster a nod.

Apeinstein studied the bird a final time then said quietly, "You need to come with me"...

CHAPTER 21
Percy's Warning

"BEN, LOOK! WE'RE ALMOST AT THE SUMMIT,"

Screamed Little John as he and Big Ben clambered up the steep rocky landscape. It was around noon on the fifth day since Plush, Peter, and Bongo had escaped their prison. After three days of trekking through dense jungle and climbing sharp, jagged rock-covered mountains with no clean water, little to no food, and all the while sporting multiple injuries worthy of the ER, Big Ben and Little John were beyond exhausted.

Their box of protein bars had barely lasted them a day. And, having no idea if the many plants around them were safe for human consumption, they didn't dare eat the unknown fruits. Big Ben suggested that they drink river water which caused both of them to get very painful stomach aches along with vomiting and high fevers. Thirsty, hungry, and sick, the two humans somehow kept moving.

Using the shotgun they salvaged from the wreck, they shot a small gazelle wandering around the base of the mountains. However, after killing the small animal, Ben and John realized they had no way to cook it since all the dead wood and leaves for miles had been soaked by rainwater. In anguish, they left the gazelle and kept moving, doing their best to ignore the ever-growing pains in their stomachs.

They also had to abandon some of their belongings at the base of the mountain including their tent, their sleeping bags, their backpacks, and their hunting jackets. With their physical limitations, it would be impossible to drag the gear up the mountain. They had spent the last two nights in the open air, taking turns sleeping while the other kept watch. It was misery.

Thankfully, the two battered men had the tracker, and it seemed Plush was still heading back towards his savannah in the southern part of Shimba Hills National Park where Ng'ombe Miji was located. Since the village offered the closest human presence for dozens of miles, it was also the best option for Big Ben and Little John's survival. Little John still had his smartphone and a portable phone charger, so they were able to use their tracker. However, they were hundreds of miles from the nearest cell tower so apart from the tracker, Little John's phone was utterly useless.

After reaching the top of the mountain, they had to descend the other side which was less steep but much more dense with trees and plants. The idea of going back into a swampy, humid hell was extremely depressing for the two humans, and they both stopped to rest trying to enjoy the view and cooler air before they entered the dark, wet woods.

Little John had taken his phone out and, after cutting himself on the cracked screen, managed to unlock it. He opened the tracker app and gasped, nearly dropping his phone in shock.

"What is it, John?" said Big Ben, uninterested.

Little John didn't seem able to talk, instead he walked over to his companion and shoved the phone into Big Ben's hand. Big Ben glanced down at the cracked screen and actually dropped the phone. If the tracker was telling the truth then it looked like Plush was...

"He's just down there at the base of the mountain...that's less than a kilometer away... but that's crazy! He was at least a dozen kilometers ahead of us this morning!" said Big Ben, his voice too shocked to yell.

"What should we do?" asked Little John, readying an arrow on his bow.

Big Ben did not respond, he just stared at the ground (he didn't even pick up the dropped phone).

Little John repeated his question, "BEN, what are we going to do? Should we go after him?"

Big Ben stood up, raised his pump-action, sawed-off shotgun, and loaded it. Big Ben picked up the smartphone and turned to face Little John. And as primal determination lit up his face, he said, "JOHN, LET'S GO

Shouting with excitement the two men began stumbling down the mountain, unaware of the small parrot circling above them, watching as they rushed towards the unsuspecting animals.

✳✳

"YOU DID WHAT?" roared Peter and Bongo at the exact same time.

Plush stared guiltily at the ground. "I already told you," muttered Plush. His voice, though soft and sad, was starting to show mild annoyance. "I sent Percy to deliver a message to my dying grandfather. What else do you want to know?" asked Plush. "I don't know why you guys care so much. Percy told me the quickest way for us to get back to the savannah, and, besides, he will be back any time now."

From the tone of his voice, Peter knew Plush didn't think he did anything unreasonable and tried to understand the logic behind sending their guide off to be a mail bird.

"Plush, you said it yourself: sending a message back to your forest was a fool's errand," said Peter. "There is just not enough proof to convince a tribe of stubborn baboons that the apes are not responsible for Bongo's disappearance unless you and Bongo tell them in person."

Once again, Plush knew Peter was right, but he would never let Peter know that; instead, he changed the subject, asking a question of his own. "I don't understand why you care so much, Peter. You're free now. The humans are out of our lives forever. Why are you still helping us? I mean, what's in it for you? You could just slither away, go off on your own, and start a new life."

Peter looked taken aback, and his eyes glared at Plush with anger and annoyance. "Don't change the subject. I promised to help you escape and get back home. That promise is not completed until you're back in your savannah," said Peter, his raspy voice hissing with anger.

Plush was about to snap back when suddenly he was distracted by the sound of something crashing and smashing through the trees above them.

A mass of gray feathers came hurtling out of the sky towards them; it flew right at Plush. He ducked as the object bounced off his head and collapsed on the ground. An instant later, he realized who the object was.

"PERCY! WHAT HAPPENED? ARE YOU ALRIGHT?" said Plush, rubbing his bruised head.

The small parrot didn't seem badly injured, but he was panting and gasping for air. Percy's face was bright red from exhaustion. He had clearly been flying very far, very fast. But as Plush stared at the bird, he knew that something else was wrong.

The bird was shaking with something other than exhaust: it was fear. Pure terror was in Percy's eyes, and as Plush and Peter looked at each other in confusion, they saw that Percy was trying to say something between his weary gasps for air.

Percy felt his vision begin to darken, and he knew he was about to pass out from exhaustion, but he had to warn his friends. Somehow he managed to find the strength to pause between gasps and mutter a single word:

"RUN..."

CHAPTER 22
The Crazy Cursed Collar

The two men stumbled down the mountain and through the forest moving as quickly as they could. The trees were dense, and the ground was covered with bushes, plants, and roots. The thick canopy blocked most of the sunlight, so it was relatively dim. After about five minutes, the terrain flattened out.

"Ben, stop!" said Little John as his arm reached out, stopping his companion.

Little John pointed ahead towards the distant treeline. Big Ben spotted what Little John was looking at. A small clearing was ahead, and the two humans could see three distant figures. They knew they had found their escaped animals.

"Quiet. Don't move a muscle," said Little John.

Little John turned just in time to see Big Ben raise his shotgun at the distant figure of Plush; he was about to pull the trigger.

"NOO!" screamed Little John, and he lunged at Big Ben and grabbed the gun.

"BEN, WHAT ARE YOU DOING? MR. WINSON NEEDS THE APE ALIVE!" screamed Little John.

He tried to snatch the gun away from Big Ben, but his larger companion shoved him back, and Little John lost his balance and fell.

Big Ben looked like he was on the verge of insanity. The events of the last week seemed to have driven all sense from his mind. "I DON'T CARE, JOHN. I DON'T CARE ANYMORE! AFTER EVERYTHING THAT APE HAS PUT US THROUGH, I AM NOT GOING TO LET IT LIVE," screamed Big Ben, he took aim and fired at Plush.

BLAM!

Plush yelled and spun around as the bark from a nearby tree exploded everywhere. Plush, Bongo, and Peter stared at each other for a split second, then they all screamed simultaneously.

"RUUUUNNNNN!"

Plush scooped the unconscious Percy into his arms and ran.

Plush was tearing through the dense trees, not daring to look back, not daring to stop--not even to figure out which way he was going; he ran and he ran. The trees were a blur of green as he sped through the jungle. He heard several gunshots in the distance, but they seemed far away.

The ape's mind was racing.

"How did they survive their crash? How did they find us? HOW? HOW?"

Several times he thought he saw glimpses of figures moving in the corner of his eyes, but he couldn't make them out, and he would not stop running until he knew he had put a considerable distance between himself and the humans. Then, up ahead, Plush spotted a massive boulder the size of a large house in his path.

Plush clambered over the rock and collapsed on the other side. It was a decent hiding spot. Plush curled up behind the massive stone, still clutching the half-dead Percy.

The forest was silent, no birds, no insects, no wind; it seemed as if all the earth was holding its breath. The only sound Plush could hear was his own frantic heartbeat.

Where were Bongo and Peter? Had he left them behind to be picked off by the humans?

Plush took several deep breaths; it didn't seem the humans were anywhere nearby. Percy was still asleep, and Plush was starting to calm down. His desperate gasps for air had subsided, and he began feeling drowsy. Plush tried to remain alert and conscious, but utter exhaustion from surviving the worst week of his life seemed to be winning. Finally, Plush closed his eyes and felt himself slowly drift off to sleep.

✳✳

Bongo was flying through the treetops, swinging from tree to tree with great speed. Below him, on the ground, he heard the thumping footsteps of Big Ben, who was charging through the dense terrain, chasing what he thought was Plush through the dense, dark woods. It was late afternoon now, and the sun was starting to set over the horizon. When Big Ben had fired at Plush, Bongo had clambered up a tree and attempted to hide in the canopy, but he sneezed loudly due to the tree being a banana tree. He realized he had given his position away and made a mad dash from tree to tree, cursing his banana allergies. He had no idea where Plush, Percy, and Peter were. Eventually, he was able to find refuge in a tall bush and watched fearfully as the enraged human ran past him into the woods. Breathing a sigh of relief, he cautiously crept from his hiding space, but then out of the corner of his eyes, he saw something and dived back into the bush, and not a moment too soon. Little John came limping out of the tree line and rushed right by the bush Bongo was hiding in. Little

John shouted something in human form that Bongo didn't understand. Once the smaller human had also run out of sight, Bongo cautiously left his hiding space and tiptoed through the woods. It was getting darker now, and Bongo was completely lost.

****

"Plush, Plush, wake up, wake UP," said Percy, whimpering as he aggressively pecked the sleeping ape on the head. He didn't dare shout, knowing the humans could be anywhere around them. Plush opened his eyes and jumped up so suddenly he banged his head on the looming mass of the boulder behind him.

"*I'm awake, I'm awake,*" hissed Plush, and he shooed Percy away with his arms.

"Hey, Ape, what happened? Where are Bongo and the snake guy, Phil?"

"You mean Peter? The python's name is Peter, *not* Phil."

Percy shrugged, and suddenly without warning, his eyes widened, and he shouted.

"PLUSH, THE HUMANS! THEY'RE HERE! ALIVE! AND THEY HAVE BEEN FOLLOWING YOU FOR..."

Plush clamped his hands over Percy's beak before he could shout another word.

"Be quiet, be quiet. Are you trying to get us found? I know humans are here. It's the reason we're hiding behind this rock. I grabbed you after you passed out and carried you to safety--something I'm kind of starting to regret," growled Plush, as he slowly lowered his hands from the parrot's beak. The parrot nodded, and then it was Plush's turn to ask a question.

"Percy, how did you know the humans were after us?" said Plush looking suspiciously at the bird.

"I was flying back from delivering your message; I didn't know exactly how far you guys had traveled, so I was circling the mountain for hours, and, lucky I did, because after three hours of circling nonstop, guess who I spotted rushing down the mountain right towards the densest area of the forest? It's almost as if humans have some sort of magic power that lets them know where you are at all times!"

Plush stared at the parrot for some time before he said anything else.

"Percy, I think you might be onto something; think about it. They have been following us for days, and somehow, they know where we are all the time. It doesn't make sense. how could they do that?"

Plush's racing mind was interrupted by the sound of something moving nearby. Plush could hear snapping twigs and footsteps...

Someone or something was creeping around on the opposite side of the boulder. Plush silently snatched a branch lying on the ground, and with Percy on his shoulder, he cautiously crept around the back of the huge rock, ready to whack and smack and fight for his life.

There was nobody there; it was just the other side of the large rock. Plush and Percy glanced at each other, confused. They had definitely heard something moving right there. If the creature--whatever it was--had started moving around the opposite side of the boulder or moved away from it, they would have heard it.

Then with a sudden realization, Plush knew where the mysterious stalker must be. Plush had just enough time to whisper, "Percy, it's right above us," before a figure came leaping off the top of the large boulder and came crashing towards them. Before Plush could do anything, a bunch of bananas slammed onto his head. Plush, dazed from the blow, lost his balance and fell.

"FEAR ME--ACHOO--AND FEAR MY TAIL, YOU HORRIBLE--ACHOO--HOMO SAPIENS. "

Bongo stood over him, wielding a massive bundle of bananas in each hand and his tail was blindly slamming the mounds of fruit over Plush's head. Plush felt his fear turn to annoyance as he tried to shout between the merciless banana batterings. "BONGO STOP! IT'S ME! IT'S PLUSH, YOU IDIOT," yelled Plush.

Bongo stopped his attack at the sight of Plush and helped the dazed ape to his feet.

"Oh, it's just you. Sorry, I thought you were a human; my bad," said Bongo.

Plush got up; his face was covered with the mashed remains of bananas. Plush longed to strike Bongo with his tree branch. Still, he decided against it, knowing the noise could attract the humans even though they had likely already heard Bongo's ranting.

"Bongo, what happened? Where is Peter?" muttered Plush trying to be as silent as possible.

Bongo shrugged. "I don't know. Where is he?" he asked.

Plush glared at him with deep annoyance. "Why would I ask you where Peter was if I already KNEW?" said Plush trying to shout as quietly as possible.

The two primates and one bird remained hiding next to the massive boulder for quite a while. The sun had started to set and the sky was gradually darkening. Plush had no idea what they were going to do once night struck. He had considered going to look for Peter using the darkness to their advantage, but the snake could be anywhere by now, and the humans were still wandering around. Bongo and Percy were no help at all; they sat in the shadow of the massive rock playing *I Spy*.

"Would you two stop messing around? We need to find Peter, and we need to keep moving," said Plush. Plush realized that in hiding from the humans, they had delayed themselves an entire evening of walking.

His thoughts were interrupted by Bongo standing up and tapping Plush on the shoulder repeatedly. "Uh, Plush..." said Bongo nervously.

"What is it Bongo? I am trying to think of a plan," said Plush, confident that anything Bongo wanted to tell him would be useless.

"Uh, Plush, is it just me, or is that log coming towards us?" said Bongo shaking with fear.

This statement was so absurd it took Plush several seconds to comprehend what Bongo had said.

"Logs can't move, Bongo," said Plush. He tried to return to his thoughts, but a moment later Bongo tapped on Plush's shoulder, again frantically pointing at something behind him. Plush raised his shoulders in exasperation and turned, jumping with shock. It wasn't Bongo's imagination.

What Plush had taken as a fallen tree was now curling and uncurling itself, relieving Peter the Python of his clever disguise: he had covered himself in mud and pretended to be a log.

"Peter, what on earth?"

"*No time for questions, follow me, and be quiet,*" said Peter. Together the group set off quickly and quietly moving in single file (except for Percy who took flight flying just over the treetops as lookout).

By now, the sun had fully set, and it was pitch black in the woods. The forest was dark and eerily quiet. It was dawning on Plush that in all their journey, they had seen very few animals in these woods. But silence was an advantage. Plush's sharp ears remained alert and focused as they kept moving. The jungle was his friend, his ally. He had lived in a forest his entire life; it was his natural habitat. The humans were outsiders to the natural world.

"Hey, Peter," said Plush.

"What?" the snake responded.

"Do you know how the humans were able to find us? I mean, they seem to know our general location regardless of distance."

Peter sighed deeply and turned to face his younger friend.

"Humans are strange, mysterious, and powerful creatures. There are things about them even I don't know. I am afraid this is one of those things."

"But you must have some idea or theory behind their powers," said Plush.

Peter thought. Although his years of imprisonment had taught him many things about humans, in the end he was still just a snake and couldn't possibly ever fully understand their mysteries. He wasn't even sure if the humans could understand all of their OWN mysteries.

He was about to respond with another uncertain answer when he caught sight of the leather collar on Plush's neck. He had noticed it before but had not given it any thought. Now a funny feeling was growing inside him, and he was sure there was much more to the small object tied to Plush's neck than met the eye.

"Wait! Plush! The collar! The one on your neck! I just remembered!"

"What?' said Plush, confused.

"Well, Plush, remember the moving-eye monsters that the humans called cameras that were in our cell?" said Peter, speaking quickly.

"Yeah," said Plush, confused. "I remember those, Peter. What do they have to do with anyth..."

Peter cut Plush off, practically shouting with realization.

"REMEMBER HOW THE HUMANS..."

"Quiet!" said Plush frantically waving his arms.

"Sorry," whispered Peter. "Anyway, Plush, do you remember how the humans could use the camera things to somehow know what we were doing at all times? Well, I think your crazy cursed collar might have some sort of human dark magic on it that lets them know where the wearer is at all times!" said Peter who was nearly bursting with pride over his own intelligence.

Plush was shocked at how quickly Peter had put two and two together. "So what do we do now?" said Plush, hoping Peter would have the answer; however, it was Bongo who spoke first.

"I vote we sacrifice Plush as a diversion. He will distract the humans while the rest of us escape. They're really only after him, not the rest of us," said Bongo in a perfectly casual voice.

All eyes turned to Bongo, and after in uncomfortable silence, he realized he must have said something upsetting.

"I was just kidding," he muttered unconvincingly.

"If anyone is going to be sacrificed, it should be YOU, Monkey. You're the least useful one in this group," said Plush angrily.

"No one is getting sacrificed, Primates," said Peter in a commanding voice.

"Who made YOU king of the Monkey, Ape, Parrot, and Python Club?" said Bongo.

"I did," said Peter. Bongo looked cross but didn't press the subject. Peter continued, "Now if you two mammals are finished bickering, then LISTEN UP. First things first: Plush, we need to get the collar off you."

Unfortunately, that was easier said than done. At first they tried pulling the collar off Plush. When that didn't work, they tried biting the collar, ripping the collar, and stretching the collar. They kept moving, stopping every couple of minutes to make another vain attempt at removing the collar. Nothing worked. After hours of trying with no success, they had to keep moving. Plush felt a mounting hopelessness rise within him.

What if he could never get the collar off? What if he had to live the rest of his life knowing the humans knew exactly where he was?

His thoughts were interrupted by an unexpected turn of events: Bongo tripped, causing him to bump against Peter who fell back and crashed on top of Plush.

Plush fell backwards onto the ground and felt something click near his neck, causing the tightness he felt around his throat to vanish.

He stood up and saw the collar lying on the ground! Apparently, there was a button on the back of it which they had completely missed; when Plush had fallen over, the force of the button hitting the ground caused the collar to unbuckle and free him.

Plush picked up the collar, looking in confusion at Bongo and Peter. "We just wasted hours trying to get that thing off, and all along WE JUST HAD TO PUSH A STUPID BUTTON!!"

"So what happens now?" asked Percy.

"We need to destroy that collar," said Peter.

"Oooooo, can I do it?" said Bongo excitedly. Without waiting for a response, he rushed off into the woods and returned moments later, carrying a rock the size of a watermelon. He placed the collar on the ground and raised the rock over his head ready to smash the tangle of wires and plastic to pieces. However, at the last second Plush jumped forward and shouted, "WAIT!!"

CHAPTER 23
The Trap

Jumping forward and shouting turned out to be a mistake. The sudden movement surprised Bongo, and he jumped back in shock and dropped the massive rock which landed right on Plush's foot.

"OW, OW, OW!" shouted Plush as he hopped on one foot, holding the other in his arms.

Bongo, Peter, and Percy looked at each other with a mixture of sympathy and confusion.

"Plush, what do you mean? Of course, we need to destroy this thing," said Peter.

Plush stopped hopping and turned to face his friends, still wincing in pain and rubbing his injured foot.

"Here me out, guys. We can't destroy it yet. Even if the humans don't know our exact location, they have probably already figured out where we're going. Right now, they are tired, starving, injured, and at their weakest. We might not get another chance, but I think...no, *I know*, we need to stop running. We need to use the collar to lure them in. We need to **FIGHT**..."

"WHAT? ARE YOU CRAZY?" said Bongo.

"We don't stand a chance! They have weapons of terrible power," said Peter.

"You think I don't know that?" said Plush, slightly put out by their lack of understanding. However, he was far from giving up.

"We know the land; they don't. We could ambush them. Take away their weapons, and physically they're relatively weak. They're not as strong as you and me, Peter. They are not as fast as you, Bongo. And, Percy....um...I will get back to that later. Look, if we run, we might escape them for a time, but they will just be back. Maybe even in greater numbers. We outnumber them now, and we might never get another chance like this. The humans are at their weakest--you saw them. They are both terribly thin and sickly looking, but we are strong and healthy. We have plenty of food, while they have none. We have water, but they looked parched and dehydrated. We are in our natural environment. We know the land, they don't," Plush finished talking. He waited for a response from one of his friends, but none came. Peter was frowning, thinking hard, weighing the chances. Bongo was looking uncomfortable and slightly scared, and Percy was giving Plush a look that plainly said, "NOPE."

"Look, I am going to fight with or without your help," said Plush. "If you don't want to help me, fine. Leave. Say goodbye now because you're probably never going to see me again."

Plush turned and walked away, feeling a kind of determined calm rise within him.

"Hey, Ape, wait!" said a voice.

Plush turned. Peter was slithering towards him, also looking determined.

186

"Our chances are not very good, but..." he hissed deeply. "Well, luck's been on our side all the way up to now. Maybe it will continue."

Plush couldn't help himself; he rushed forward and hugged the massive snake. "Thank you," whispered Plush.

Bongo stepped forward and Plush realized it was the first time he had ever seen Bongo looking even slightly serious.

"Ok, I'm in, but if we die, Plush, it's your fault!"

"So, Ape, what's the plan?" said Peter.

Plush was taken aback at this. He had gotten used to following Peter around, letting him make the decisions. Peter had always been the self-appointed leader of their group, but now, here he was asking *Plush* to make the plan. Plush was not entirely sure what he was going to do; he thought back to the time when the humans captured him, the time when he had snuck into the cow field ALONE trying to prove himself. It seemed so long ago, and it was hard to comprehend that little over a week ago, he had been living his normal life in the savannah. But now, everything was different. He was not alone. He was part of a team--a weird team, an imperfect team, an unlikely team--but a team, nonetheless.

"I know what we need to do," said Plush confidentiality.

"WE are going to make a TRAP."

Suddenly, Plush realized Percy was still there.

The parrot was looking uncomfortable, trying to give a smile that didn't quite shield the fear in his eyes

"Well, good luck you guys," he chuckled nervously.

"Um...you know, I JUST remembered I gotta be somewhere. I'll...uh... catch up with you later."

He raised his wings and was about to take flight when he spoke again.

"Oh, and, Plush, I almost forgot to tell you. Your grandfather woke up from his coma and is recovering. Anyway....um...bye."

The parrot took flight, zooming away into the distance. Plush stood shocked for a moment then shouted at the distant bird. "PERCY, GET BACK HERE! YOU CHICKEN!! WAIT! WHAT HAPPENED WITH MY GRANDFATHER?" he roared, but the small bird was already flying away, a speck far out into the horizon. Soon, he was out of sight.

"That tiny coward!" roared Plush kicking the ground.

Peter spoke sympathetically, "Listen ape it's not Percy's fight. He was not a prisoner to the humans like we were. He agreed to help us, and he has done more than we ever expected of him. Besides, he's a two-pound parrot. What help would he be in a fight?"

Plush sighed deeply and looked around scanning the nearby woods. Up ahead of them, illuminated by the moonlight, was a small grassy hill with a cluster of trees and bushes on top.

"I got it! I know what to do," said Plush enthusiastically.

He led the group to the clearing and began brainstorming the plan of attack.

"Ok, here's what we should do," he said as he placed the collar in the middle of the clearing and looked at Peter.

"Peter, you climb up those trees and try to blend in when the humans come through. As soon as you see them, you jump down on top of them just as Bongo and I rush out from the bushes here." He pointed to a thick cluster of bushes on the edge of the clearing. "If the plan works, they can come from any direction and we'll still be attacking them from above and around them."

Plush, Peter, and Bongo got into position. Peter slithered up the tree and out onto the branches, stretching over the open ground beneath him. Plush and Bongo had a more difficult time concealing themselves in the bushes. Bongo yelped loudly every time he got poked by a sharp leaf and kept trying to reposition himself, causing the bush to shake dramatically until he finally found a semi-comfortable position.

"So what do now?" said Bongo, his voice showing no sign of fear, only boredom.

Plush stared into the monkey's eyes amazed to see no fear in them. "We wait."

And so they waited and waited as the night wore on and the moon rose higher and higher into the sky. The only sounds were the occasional chirping of an insect or a gust of wind against the tree branches.

Thoughts began to race through Plush's mind. What if the humans didn't show up? What if they did, but the trap failed? Plush or one of his friends could be killed. Plush was aware that in choosing to fight the humans they were rapidly losing time to get back to his savannah before Bongo's birthday and the baboon attack. The baboon tribe would kill all of Plush's tribe, and in the following days, the northern apes would kill all of the unsuspecting baboons. It was a truly depressing thought. Part of Plush felt angry at his own lack of sympathy for Bongo's tribe. In truth, he couldn't care less if they *were* wiped out. He liked Bongo as a friend and knew the baboons thought the apes had killed their king's son, but the baboons had been attacking the apes for years--well before Bongo was born and probably even before his grandfather was born. And even if he could somehow save his own tribe but allowed the northern apes to destroy Bruno's tribe, where would that leave Bongo? He'd be without a family, and Plush knew he could never do that to his friend, no matter how annoying he was. Even if he could prove the apes were not behind Bongo's disappearance, what if the baboons did not care and continued with their plan?

Plush tried to turn his thoughts back towards the immediate threat of the two humans; dawn would be approaching in the next few hours, and he hoped the humans would appear soon before the sun rose, when it would be much more likely for them to notice the trap. What if their theory about the collar had been wrong?

Plush did his best to block these thoughts from his mind and keep his head in the game. Dawn was really starting to show itself now. A pink streak was visible in the east. As the sky brightened, Plush felt his mood darken. The humans were nowhere to be found. He was about to stand up and call to Peter when his ears caught the sound of something, and he dove back into the bush.

Glancing at Bongo, he whispered, "Shh...they're coming." And coming, they were! The voices of Big Ben and Little John were clearly audible through the air. And they were coming from the base of the hill in front of them although they weren't visible yet as the hill was too steep to see the bottom from where they were hiding. Plush waited for them to appear, listening in on their conversation. Which he found he could once again understand.

Little John was laughing loudly, his voice carrying through the air, "Ha! Hey, Ben, listen to this. I found this news article right before we got out of service range. Apparently, the same day our ape escaped, dozens of people back in Nairobi called the police saying they saw a chimpanzee running through the city, yelling curse words and terrorizing people. HA! It says here the police say it was a crazy person in an ape costume, and they are looking for a short male of unknown race with a eastern European accent. Looks like they turned our chimp into a talking man in a monkey suit!"

"That's ridiculous," Big Ben said, not finding it funny.

"Apes don't talk. It reminds of those superstitious villagers who thought demons were stealing their cows. Idiots!"

Something they said rang a bell in Plush's ear, and he had a funny feeling the crazy, short guy with the accent was actually him (though, of course, he did not find it funny.)

The two humans came into view. Big Ben was in front followed by Little John. They looked terrible; their clothes were torn in places and filthy. They were thin and sickly- looking. Their arms and legs were covered in dirt, cuts, bruises, and mud. They both looked weak and tired, hungry and thirsty. But more than anything, Plush noticed that the human eyes were filled with fury and hate for the creatures that had given them such trouble. It was clear that any previous desire to capture Plush alive was no more. Only a murderous hatred existed in the tired weak- bodied humans.

Despite their haggard appearance, Big Ben still had his sawed off shotgun and Little John had his bow and several arrows strapped to his back.

"John, check the tracker see if the ape is anywhere nearby," said Big Ben.

Plush waited, feeling the adrenaline build up inside him; he just had to wait for them to catch sight of their collar, which was placed directly underneath the large branch that was really Peter the python. "Come on a few more steps," whispered Plush.

Next to him, Bongo had, of course, fallen asleep. Plush decided against trying to wake him up, knowing that any noise of surprise from Bongo could give their location away. Plush waited, listening as Little John spoke, "Ben, it looks like the ape is right here," said Little John.

"Oh, great! That ape could be hiding a kilometer in any direction. Seriously, this is RIDICULOUS!" He stopped talking. To Plush's horror, he saw the large human snap his eyes in Plush and Bongo's direction. He was staring right at them--only a wall of leaves hid them from view.

"He must have heard something," thought Plush. Big Ben started walking towards the bush. Plush felt his heart practically jumping with anticipation. But then he saw that Big Ben was not looking at him. The human bent down and picked up the collar. Little John joined him. Big Ben was fuming, his face turning a deep red.

"BLOODY HELL! THE DAMN APE GOT OUT OF HIS..."

CRASH!

The two humans looked up to see Peter the Python crashing down from the tree branch above them. They both jumped back in shock. Little John, whose leg was still injured from the car crash, lost his balance and fell. Unable to steady himself on the uneven ground, he went plummeting down the hill; he came to a stop at its base, dazed but relatively unharmed. Big Ben barely had time to blink before Plush came charging out of the bush towards him.

Instinctively, Big Ben raised his shotgun at Plush, but Peter leapt forward, flipped his head sideways, opened his mouth wide, and sank his teeth into the side of Big Ben just above his waist. The sudden attack caused Big Ben to lose his balance and fall over. As he fell, his fingers clenched the trigger causing it to fire. The rounds flew over Plush's head striking the trees behind him. The sudden gunshots dazed Plush, momentarily slowing him.

Big Ben was yelling and screaming as Peter began to strangle him, wrapping his massive coils around the large human. Big Ben was too busy trying to wrestle the massive snake off him; he didn't see Plush. Peter raised his head high into the air.

"SO HUNGRY!" he announced, though all Big Ben heard was hissing. The snake opened his mouth wide, ready to deliver the final blow against the creatures who had tortured him for over ten years, but suddenly there was a loud *whizzing* noise and an arrow went flying through the air right into the side of Peter's neck.

192

With a terrible "HISSSSS!" the injured python leapt back, writhing in pain. Plush turned to see Little John limping back up the hill, already loading another arrow in his bow.

Before Plush could regain control of the situation, Big Ben was already back on his feet. With a roar of rage, the big man slammed the butt of his shotgun against Plush's head.

Plush stumbled backwards. His vision went foggy and his head swam. Big Ben raised his shotgun, not at Plush, but at the writhing mass of Peter.

"NO!" Plush leapt at the human, but not before he heard the deafening BANG and another terrible hiss of pain as the slugs of a shotgun went flying into Peter's stomach.

Plush lunged at Big Ben and punched him in his already wounded side. Big Ben yelled in pain and swung his shotgun at Plush, knocking the ape back. Plush lost his balance and fell. He looked up to see Big Ben raise the shotgun right to his face. At point-blank range there was no way Plush would survive. Peter was curled into a ball. Due to his size, he was not mortally wounded, but he was unable to continue fighting.

By now, Little John had reached the top of the hill and started kicking the bleeding Peter, yelling, "I HATE SNAKES! I HATE SNAKES!"

It seemed like the battle was lost, and the only member of the group unharmed was hiding in the bushes.

Bongo was awake at this point and was watching the carnage from the safety of his hiding space; he was petrified with fear.

"What do I do, what do I do, what do I do?" he muttered, frantically trying to regain control of his paralyzed body.

Suddenly, Bongo heard a small voice coming from his left. *"Save Plush,"* said the voice. Bongo turned and saw, standing on his shoulder, what could only be described as a mini-Bongo. The figure stood about two inches tall but was the spitting image of Bongo himself. *"Save Plush,"* the figure repeated, in a voice identical to his own.

Before Bongo could respond, he heard another voice, this time coming from his right. *"Save Peter,"* Bongo turned and saw another mini version of himself standing on his right shoulder. Before Bongo could shout, "What in the world?" He heard another voice, this one coming from the top of his head. *"Leave Peter, leave Plush, save yourself."* Though Bongo couldn't see the source of the noise, he was sure that there was another Bongo on top of his head.

"What in my tail's name is going on, who are you mini-mes?" said Bongo, suspiciously staring from one shoulder to another.

"We're just figments of your imagination here to help you deal with stress," said the first mini-Bongo.

"Now SAVE PLUSH," roared the first mini-Bongo right in

his ear.

"NO!" the second Bongo responded. *"LEAVE PLUSH; SAVE PETER!"*

"NO! LEAVE THEM BOTH! SAVE YOURSELF!" yelled the third voice.

The voices of his imaginary mini triplets rang in Bongo's head, their advice echoing louder and louder. He yelled in misery, trying to cover his ears, he began to roll around shaking on the ground in a violent fit. Clearly, he was in no position to save his friends.

Meanwhile, Big Ben had his gun pointed right at Plush's face, and ignoring the movement coming from the shaking bushes, he let out a mad laugh and pulled back the spring.

Suddenly, there was a loud screaming "SQUWAAAAAAK!" and a blur of something gray and feathery shot through the air, flying right at Big Ben's face.

"P...PERCY! YOU CAME BACK!" said Plush, amazed and frozen in shock.

"I KNEW YOU WOULD BE LOST WITHOUT ME, APE. DON'T WORRY! I GOT THIS!" yelled Percy.

The small bird slammed into the human's face, smacking Big Ben with his wings and scratching him with his claws. Big Ben was waving his free arm trying to shoo the bird away. Plush was still too dazed to get to his feet as his head was still swimming.

"JOHN, GET THIS PIGEON OFF ME!" yelled Big Ben, covering his face as Little John rushed over to assist him.

"SHOO! SHOO, YOU FILTHY ANIMAL!" yelled Little John, and he whacked Percy with his bow sending the bird spirling backward into the air.

Without any hesitation, Big Ben aimed his shotgun at Percy, and pulled the trigger...

CHAPTER 24
An Easy Kill

BLAM!

Plush screamed in horror--a scream that was drowned out by the bellowing roar of the gun.

There was an explosion of feathers as Percy the Parrot fell out of the sky, his limp body crashing down at Plush's feet.

Time seemed to slow down for Plush. His mind froze. He was unable to think, unable to comprehend what had just happened. He saw Big Ben raise the shotgun at him and heard the human shout, "ADIOS, APE."

Big Ben pulled the trigger and Plush knew there was no way he was going to survive. He closed his eyes and calmly accepted his fate as he waited for death to claim him.

Nothing happened.

Plush opened his eyes and saw that Big Ben was cursing in anger as he grappled with the gun in his hands. He was out of bullets.

As this realization occurred to Plush, he felt his survival instincts return, and from the pit of his soul a hatred more powerful than anything he had ever felt in his life welled up within him.

Plush felt his **anger** turn to **hate**, his **hate** turn to **rage** and his **rage** turn to **POWER.**

Little John saw Plush charge at him and Big Ben.

Little John laughed and fired an arrow at Plush.

Plush saw the arrow, and he felt his body move seemingly on its own. Instead of dodging the deadly projectile, the ape's long arm lunged out, and he seized the arrow midair. Little John barely had time to blink in horror before he felt the searing pain of Plush stabbing the arrow deep into his already-injured leg.

"AHHHH!!" Little John screamed, in a mixture of pain, anger, and shock. He tried to hit Plush with his bow, but Plush was too quick for him. Plush wrenched the bow out of Little John's grip with ease and swung it across the ground, knocking Little John's legs out from under him. Little John lost his balance and fell on his back. Big Ben tried to intervene, raising his shotgun at Plush, but before he could strike, Plush spun around and with all of his might, punched Big Ben in the throat. Big Ben stumbled back, gagging and gasping for air. Plush turned back to Little John who screamed and tried to kick Plush with his uninjured leg. But the ape was too quick. Like lightning, Plush leapt into the air and slammed the metal bow against Little John's chest with such force that the bow snapped in two.

Little John didn't even scream--probably because he had no air left in his lungs. He let out a moan and curled into the fetal position, covering his head with his arms.

It was then that Bongo rushed out from the bushes. He picked up the bloody remains of Percy, ran out of the clearing deep into the woods, and away from the fight.

Big Ben was backing down the hill now, not taking his eyes off Plush. He was in shock after seeing Plush grab a speeding arrow out of the air. He was not taking any chances. He clutched the empty shotgun with both hands like a baseball bat ready to whack, pound, and beat Plush to death.

The side of Ben's chest was bleeding aggressively, and the pain was unbearable. Pythons have strong jaws, and Big Ben was pretty sure some of his ribs were broken from Peter's bite. Had the situation not been so tense, he would have been tempted to lie down and simply wait for some non-existent rescue.

But as Plush charged down the hill towards him, Big Ben felt a feeling of pure primal terror. He could see the ape's eyes, and it scared him beyond sense. It took all of his will-power not to drop his gun and make a run for it. In all his years of poaching, he had never seen an animal this enraged before. It was almost as if it had feelings, but that was impossible, right?

There was no time to dwell on these thoughts, and Big Ben, remembering what his highschool baseball coach had taught him about swinging a bat, raised his gun two one side with both hands ready to strike.

Plush charged down the hill, roaring and screeching, and closing the distance between himself and Big Ben.

Thirty feet. Twenty feet. Fifteen feet. Ten feet...

Big Ben swung the shotgun like a baseball bat, aiming for Plush's head. He missed, but only because Plush had jumped back to avoid the blow.

Big Ben swung his makeshift club at Plush again and again not necessarily to hit him, but momentarily keeping the ape at bay. Big Ben knew the only thing keeping him out of reach of Plush's teeth and claws was his gun-turned-club. He swung again and again, blocking the enraged ape from getting close enough to strike. But Ben was getting tired. He knew he couldn't keep it up forever. It was only a matter of time before Plush would find an opening, and then it would be over. Big Ben knew that if it came down to hand-to-hand combat, he wouldn't stand a chance against an ape of any kind, even a small runty one.

Plush was so focused on ripping Big Ben apart, he didn't notice Little John, wincing in pain, inching his way down the hill. He didn't see Little John pull the arrow from his own leg, leaving enough blood to form a stream.

Little John clutched the sharp metal arrow in his hand, and crawled slowly towards Plush. Little John was ready to return the favor.

Plush finally found his opening. As the exhausted Big Ben swung his club, Plush ducked down and launched himself forward, colliding with Big Ben's chest and knocking the large human down. The ape and human rolled down the hill, each trying to rip the other apart.

Before Big Ben knew what had happened, Plush was on top of him, pounding him in the face with all of his might. Big Ben was yelling, crying, and screaming. He knew he was not going to win a fist fight against Plush. This rage-filled ape, though young and small, was much stronger and much faster than any human.

As Plush struck Ben again and again, images began to flash through his mind. *The humans kidnapping him...the humans beating him...the humans beating Peter and Bongo...the hanging corpses of his parents...the dozens of unseeing ape skulls lining the shelves.* Each image fueled his rage as he struck Big Ben. He couldn't have stopped even if he wanted to; his body seemed to have overridden his mind. Plush pounded his fists against Big Ben's face again and again and again.

By now, Little John was only a few feet away from the crazed Plush. The ape was so focused on Big Ben, he didn't hear Little John wince in pain as he rose to his feet and made his move: using the arrow like a knife, Little John limped forward, but at the last second, he stumbled, sending the the sharp point deep into Plush's shoulder, not his neck where John had been aiming.

The pain did nothing but fuel Plush's rage. He spun around, grabbed Little John's arm and flipped the human over him. Little John yelled as he slammed into the ground. Plush, still clutching him by his right arm, proceeded to bend the arm backwards further and further. Little John yelled in agony and tried punching Plush with his free arm, but it didn't do anything to slow the rage-filled animal. A final bend and a loud bone-crunching SNAP filled the air. Little John shrieked in pain. The ape had broken his arm as easily as if the bone had been made of cardboard.

Little John collapsed, clutching his broken arm and his butchered leg, sobbing hysterically. Big Ben was moaning and gasping. He spat blood and several teeth out of his broken jaw, cursing Plush.

Plush stood over Big Ben ready to deliver a final blow to the throat; then he would deal with Little John. As he stared into Big Ben's eyes, he saw terror but more than that, he saw hate. But then, Plush saw something else: a reflection, a reflection of himself.

The tiny image of himself was standing over the pitiful, wounded creature, his fists raised. It was then that a final image surfaced in his mind.

This time Plush saw himself. He was lying on the ground, beaten and bloody, while the ape chief Travis stood over him ready to end his life without hesitation.

And just like that, all the rage, hatred, and anger in Plush vanished and were replaced by moral thought and emotion. And suddenly, Plush felt drained and tired. It was only then he realized he had an arrow sticking out of his shoulder.

As he stood over the human with his arm still raised, ready to strike, some small feeling in Plush's heart was telling him to stop. Moments earlier he had been intent on killing the humans, but now something was holding him back. Why, why, why couldn't he strike? Why couldn't he kill the creatures that had caused him and so many other animals so much pain? All he had to do was move his arms, but he couldn't. He tried to reason with himself. These creatures deserved it; they wouldn't have hesitated had they been in his position.

"But should I really sink to the level of these monsters?

Were they really monsters? Were they really all that different from apes? What about Percy?" thought Plush. *"The small bird had willingly risked his life to help them escape and the humans had killed him."*

Plush could feel the rage once again surge inside him.

Poor Plush was so lost in thought, debating with his emotions, he did not notice one of Big Ben's arms slinking towards his pocket, and he didn't catch the glint of silver in time.

All Plush noticed was a cruel sneer appear on Big Ben's bloodstained,partially-smashed face. Big Ben opened his mouth, spitting out another tooth. He bellowed--a loud inaudible rant. His outburst caused Plush to snap back to reality...a second too late.

There was a flash of silver, and Plush felt the blade of a hunting knife being driven into his lower stomach. His body screamed with pain. Big Ben laughed and kicked Plush off him with ease, pulling the knife out of Plush as kicked.

Unlike Little John, Big Ben's injuries were only present on the side of his chest and his face, not his limbs.

Plush crawled away from Big Ben as fast as he could. Blood gushed from the ape's open wound; he felt his vision blurring.

Big Ben's injured ribs made it too painful for him to stand. He began to crawl after Plush, knife in hand. He advanced slowly, blood covering his grinning face.

Plush tried to get to his feet, but Big Ben lunged forward and landed on top of Plush, and, using his massive body weight, he forced Plush to the ground. The big man let out a booming laugh, and clutching the knife with both hands, he plunged his blade towards the left side of Plush's chest, aiming for his heart. Plush grabbed Ben's arms by the wrists, trying to prevent the knife from piercing his chest. Big Ben was pushing the blade down with all of his strength, but

Plush's arms kept the knife at bay. They struggled this way for a while until Big Ben leaned forward in an attempt to put more weight on the blade. This was a mistake. As Big Ben adjusted himself, Plush's head came flying up, colliding with Big Ben's forehead.

The sudden movement sent the Big Ben rolling off Plush.

Big Ben saw Plush scrambling to his feet, and in a last desperate action, he lurched forward and managed to grab one of Plush's legs with both hands. He pulled, yanking Plush off balance.

Plush could feel his blinding rage starting to build up, but something else in his mind was also present: a thought. An idea. Something that would allow him to beat the humans without having to kill them.

Amazingly, Plush felt the words form in his mouth, and to the astonishment of himself and the humans, he yelled out in perfect English:

"LET ME GO, HUMAN!"

CHAPTER 25
The War Begins

Time seemed to pause as Big Ben stared wide-eyed at Plush.

Horror and disbelief filled Big Ben's eyes. He released Plush and stumbled back, gaping in terror. Plush stood up and looked at Big Ben's fear-filled face. The realization that the creature in front of him was no ordinary chimpanzee but something far more horrifying shone in his eyes and somehow Big Ben found the courage to speak.

Though he was stuttering terribly, "Th..th...those villiagers were right you.. YOU...YOU REALLY ARE A...A DEMON!" And then, summoning all his strength, Big Ben sprang to his feet. Ignoring the pain from his injured ribs, he pulled Little John to his feet, and the two humans stumbled away as fast as they could. They didn't care about revenge anymore; they didn't care about their mission; they didn't even care where they went as long as it was far, far from Plush.

They rushed away from the hill into the woods. Their panicking voices soon faded, and then they were gone.

Plush sat down on a tree stump, panting. So much had happened in the last few minutes. It was hard to process everything, but one thing was for sure: Percy the parrot was gone.

Plush suddenly remembered. Peter! He had been shot! Plush had left him lying in the clearing. Plush leapt to his feet and raced up the hill, praying that Peter had not succumbed to his injuries.

****

The sun had risen quite high by now, and the ape forest had awoken. However, there was a chill feeling in the air as the apes went about their duties in silence. The fear of an attack at any moment was keeping everyone unbearably on edge.

The grim stillness was shattered by two apes who rushed through the trees, bumping and crashing into others as they ran. Eventually, they burst through the trees and into the clearing filled with apes.

Purcellville and Albert Apenstein both gasped for breath as they finally stopped before the ape council.

Purcellville was terribly thin and sickly looking, and it appeared he could drop dead at any second.

"TRAVIS! TRAVIS! WE NEED TO TALK TO YOU!" yelled Apenstein.

Travis turned his scar-covered face towards them and glared with great dislike as the two elderly apes approached him.

"WHAT DO YOU TWO WANT? I'M A LITTLE BUSY AT THE MOMENT!" bellowed Travis.

Purcellville, exhausted, fell to his knees, panting and gasping for air. "I am way too old for this," he muttered to himself. "Travis, Plush is alive! He was captured by humans but escaped. He has found Bruno's son, Bongo. They are coming here to prove that we did not kidnap Bruno's son. The baboons are going to attack tomorrow at midnight, and the northern apes will not arrive until the day after the baboons' attack. By that time, it will be too late. There will be nothing left for the northern apes to save."

It took Travis several moments to comprehend what Purcellville had said; he was unsure whether to laugh or get angry; he decided on anger.

"HOW ON EARTH DO YOU KNOW THIS?" he snarled.

"A little bird told us," said Apenstein.

Travis's face turned purple with anger.

"DON'T JOKE WITH ME! GO AWAY, YOU FOOLS," yelled Travis.

"No! Travis, we're not joking. It actually was a little bird--a parrot messenger bird named Percy," said Purcellville. "He flew here yesterday, arriving just after I awoke from my coma, and told us this."

Travis looked around at the other council members. Each one had a more bewildered look on their face than the last.

By now, many chimps had gathered on the edges of the clearing, silently listening in.

Travis felt primal anger build inside him, but unlike Plush, Travis didn't even bother trying to control it.

"WHERE IS YOUR PROOF?" yelled Travis, much louder than was necessary as he was only five feet away from Purcellville.

At Travis' words, every ape looked over at Purcellville and Apenstein. Apenstein looked nervous, but Purcellville stepped forward to address the crowd.

"My fellow apes, I have been this tribe's elder for over twelve winters now, and I have done everything in my power to strengthen our tribe. I was the one who introduced new hunting tactics which greatly improved our hunting performance. I created the ape council as part of an advanced leadership system that would be vital for our growth. Everything I did was for the good of our tribe. I have had our best interests at heart, and now I beg of you, even if you do not understand how it could be possible, please trust me on this critical matter."

He finished speaking, and his words were followed by a silence so powerful the anticipation seemed to radiate through the clearing. Eventually, it was broken by Travis.

"SERIOUSLY? AM I THE ONLY APE HERE WHO UNDERSTANDS HOW ABSURD OUR ELDER'S STORY IS? HE CLAIMS A MYSTERIOUS PARROT TOLD HIM HIS DEAD GRANDSON IS ALIVE AND HAS RESCUED THE MISSING BABOON PRINCE. NOT ONLY THAT, HE IS ON HIS WAY HERE TO SAVE US BY STOPPING THE BABOONS FROM KILLING US--ALL LIES! AND EVEN IF IT WAS TRUE, DO YOU THINK THE BABOONS WOULD JUST CANCEL THE ATTACK? OF COURSE NOT! THEY HATE US AS MUCH AS WE HATE THEM. WE'RE FINISHED! THEY COULD ATTACK US AT ANY MOMENT. THEY COULD COME AT NIGHT, SNEAK INTO OUR FOREST WHILE WE ARE SLEEPING, AND...AND ..."

Travis's ranting came to a stop, and a terrible smile crossed his burn-marked face.

"I...I know what we must do," he muttered more to himself than the crowd. He scratched his forehead and fiddled with his long, clawed fingers, pondering his new thought while the crowds of apes watched with anticipation.

Suddenly, Travis broke the silence with laughter and howled with violent pleasure. "FELLOW CHIMPANZEES! I KNOW WHAT

WE MUST DO! THE BABOONS ALWAYS ATTACK OUR FOREST, BUT THE TIME HAS COME. WE MUST TAKE THE FIGHT TO THEM! WE SHALL ATTACK THE BABOONS ON THEIR OWN TURF!"

The forest erupted. Shrieks and growls filled the air as apes shouted, some in support of Travis, some completely against the idea.

"Silence, SILENCE!" roared Purcellville. Every eye turned to him, and his mind raced, trying to find some way to convince them to call off the attack. "TRAVIS, WHAT ABOUT THE RIVER? IT'S THE ONLY WAY INTO THE BABOON TERRITORY, AND WE CAN'T SWIM LIKE THE BABOONS. EVEN IF WE COULD CROSS THE RIVER, THIS IS A DEATH WISH. THERE ARE TOO MANY BABOONS--HUNDREDS, PROBABLY THOUSANDS! BY NOW, WHAT CHANCE DO SEVERAL DOZEN STARVING APES HAVE? OUR BEST OPTION IS TO SEND THEM A MESSAGE ABOUT BONGO, AND THEN HUNKER DOWN HERE AND..."

Travis, however, had had enough. His eyes full of rage, he raised his long arm, and with the strength of a lion and the speed of a cheetah, he hit Purcellville across the face, causing the old ape to lose his balance and fall over.

"WE ATTACK!! WE HAVE SPEARS, CLUBS, AND WEAPONS. THE BABOONS DO NOT. WE SURPRISE THEM! WE COULD WIN. IF WE WAIT HERE, WE DIE!"

"But the river," muttered a council member. "How do we cross the river?"

"EASY!" bellowed Travis. "WE CHOOSE A TREE IN OUR FOREST, CUT IT DOWN, AND AFTER SUNSET, WE HAUL IT TO THE RIVER AND USE IT AS A BRIDGE. THEN WE ATTACK THE BABOONS--CLUB THEM ALL IN THEIR SLEEP."

There was a brief pause after Travis spoke, and for one moment, Purcellville thought he might have gotten through to the apes, but then, one by one, the apes began their screeching war cry.

"KILL THE BABOONS!" yelled one chimpanzee.

"DEATH TO THE MONKEYS!" yelled another chimp.

"NO, NO! YOU MUST SEE REASON! THIS IS MADNESS!" yelled Purcellville, but the apes ignored him.

Travis, who was done listening to Purcellville's rational ways, grinned, showing his dark, misshapen teeth.

"PURCELLVILLE, WE ATTACK TONIGHT, AND I SAY WE SHOULD USE *YOUR* TREE HOME AS THE BRIDGE."

Purcellville tried to protest, but there was nothing he could do. The apes rushed around the forest, grabbing spears, clubs, and stones. One group descended upon Purcellville's tree and began to tear it up by the roots. The tree stood tall for quite a while; its roots were thick and its foundation was strong, but finally, the huge tree--which had been Purcellville's only home for over ten years--fell to the ground with a sickening smack.

The defeated elder stood in the clearing, watching the chaos unfold. He turned to Apenstein, his face filled with terror. Shaking his head, he simply muttered, "What have we done?" and walked away.

CHAPTER 26
Almost Home

Peter and Bongo had taken refuge deep in the forest. Bongo had not spoken a word. With eyes full of tears, he simply climbed up a tall tree and hid in the dense canopy. Peter, who was too banged up to climb a tree, curled up at the base and rested. He had not seen the outcome of the fight and did not know that Plush had been victorious. For all the old snake knew, the only creature he could ever have called a friend was probably dead.

So when the sound of approaching footsteps became audible, he immediately rose up, alert. When the figure came into view, he relaxed. Plush came stumbling through the trees, his left arm concealing his stab wound. Peter's mind immediately filled with questions. "Hey, Ape, the humans...what happened...?" said Peter, his voice filled with both curiosity and uncertainty.

Plush didn't answer, but instead, responded with a question of his own. "Where's Bongo? I thought he was with you," said Plush.

Peter gestured up the tree with a sad expression on his face. "That parrot really meant a lot to him," said Peter quietly so as to not further upset Bongo.

"That parrot's name was Percy," said Plush, his voice not angry, just sad and tired. He sat down next to Peter and stared glumly at the ground.

There was a long silence after these words. Peter sighed and laid down. The shotgun shells had penetrated the thick scales all over his stomach and back, but due to his massive size, the wounds were nothing more than severe splinters to him, and though they were very painful, Peter had felt much worse pain before. Nothing was more painful than a crazy Irishman who had too much to drink attacking you with a machete, thought Peter, shaking at the memory.

However, the fate of the humans was still Peter's most pressing matter. He waited for Plush to say something, but it never happened.

Eventually, the suspense was too much for Peter, and he impatiently blurted out, "Hey, Ape, I must know what happened to the humans!"

Plush sighed a very deep sigh.

"The humans are gone; they can't hurt us anymore," he said simply.

"So they're dead?" asked Peter.

The snake was so desperate for details he felt like shouting.

"The humans are gone. They were seriously injured, and I doubt they will survive long in these woods," said Plush. He didn't sound victorious, he didn't sound happy, but he didn't seem sad either. Plush seemed to be somewhere in between.

The group was too tired both physically and mentally to talk or continue their journey just yet; the only thing they could do was rest.

So the three animals rested. For hours, they rested. As the day wore on, and the sun rose high into the sky, still they sat under the tree in silence. They were only interrupted when Plush half-heartedly asked if anyone was hungry, and, as if on cue, a dozen tropical fruits dropped from the tree above them, obviously thrown by Bongo. Plush tried to thank him, but the monkey did not respond. Plush then remembered that Peter was a carnivore, but when he offered to go looking for some animal carcasses, the snake simply said, "Ape, I'm a python. We can live for months between meals, and after that gazelle the other day, I probably won't need to eat again until some time in the next four to six weeks."

Around four in the afternoon, Bongo came clambering down from the tree. His face was red from crying, but he had a determined, angry look in his eyes Plush had never seen before.

"We need to keep moving. Follow me. I know the way," said Bongo in a dry bland voice quite different from his usual voice; the monkey set off jogging into the woods. Leaving a confused Plush and Peter behind.

"How on earth would he know the way?" said Plush, confused.

"He doesn't," said Peter, annoyed. "He's just lost his mind AGAIN."

With nothing better to do, Plush and Peter followed the wayward monkey through the dense trees.

"HEY, BONGO, STOP! STOP! WE'RE LOST, YOU CRAZY MONKEY!" yelled Plush angrily.

But the monkey ignored him and disappeared into a thick cluster of bushes and out of sight. Plush swore angrily and leapt into the brush, desperate to find the grieving baboon that he had come to feel responsible for.

Bongo had come to a halt right on the other side of the brush, and when Plush clambered out of the bushes, he couldn't believe his eyes. The sight was breathtaking. The trees had vanished, the forest seemed to end with the wall of bushes behind them, and now they were facing miles and miles of grassy plains. The late afternoon sun illuminated the savannah grass, casting a golden shadow over the tan- coloured fields.

Plush couldn't believe they were back. He was back in the savannah. He was home.

"Bongo, how did you know?" said Plush weakly.

Bongo looked confused, "Know what?" said Bongo dryly, scratching his head in confusion. This was overwhelming for Plush, and Bongo's lack of understanding was too much to handle.

"HOW DID YOU KNOW THE WAY BACK? HOW DID YOU KNOW WE WERE THIS CLOSE TO OUR SAVANNAH?" yelled Plush.

"Oh, that," said Bongo.

"I was talking with some birds earlier when I was resting up in that tree," said Bongo. "They knew the area and gave me directions."

Plush sighed with extreme exhaustion. Even though they were back in familiar territory, the savannah was very large, and they were still miles from the ape and baboon lands.

An angry hiss behind Plush told him Peter had finally caught up to the group.

"IF YOU RUN AHEAD AND LEAVE ME IN THE DUST ONE MORE TIME, I SWEAR I WILL..." Peter stopped talking, his massive mouth opened wide as he took in the sight. While Plush had been gone for a little over a week, Peter hadn't laid his eye on his home in over twelve years. Both the python and ape stood in quiet reverence, overcome with emotion.

It seemed that the loss of Percy had sparked some sort of sense of purpose in Bongo, as he was the first to break the silence.

"Come on, we need to find my dad before it's too late," said Bongo.

The monkey took off running down the hill. Plush looked back at Peter. The snake looked very tired; his head was bowed down, and he was hissing softly to himself.

Plush realized Peter had finished his part of the deal. He had gotten them home and so that must mean...

"So, Peter, I guess this is goodbye," said Plush, smiling reassuringly. But the snake looked up at Plush and shook his head.

"I think I can help out a little longer. Something tells me you might need a python's help when you speak to the tribes."

CHAPTER 27
The Monkey Massacre

As soon as the sun had fully set, Travis ordered the apes to move out. Around thirty chimps grabbed the branches and trunk of what had been Purcellville's tree and began to drag the makeshift bridge toward the river. It took a surprisingly short time considering the size of the tree. However, when they reached the river, they were faced with a new challenge. Although the river was less than forty feet wide, it was still very deep in the middle, and the current was strong--too strong for an ape to wade through--and impossible for them to swim through.

(As I said before, chimpanzees can not swim.)

The apes tried many ways to hoist the tree over the river and land on the opposite bank, though it was proving a much more difficult task than they had originally believed.

It took around thirty minutes of intense heaving to finally turn the tree into a functioning bridge, though not a very reliable one. The apes had stripped all the branches and bark off the tree to make it lighter, however this made the tree very unstable--even for chimpanzees who are some of the best climbers in the world. It was difficult to cross. The tree-turned- bridge was also very narrow--so narrow, in fact, the apes had to cross in single file. This consumed an enormous amount of time as there were about eighty chimpanzees that needed to cross.

About halfway through getting all the chimpanzees on the baboon side of the river, disaster struck. The tree shifted so suddenly, half a dozen chimpanzees lost their balance and were sent plunging into the river. The terrified primates got caught in the current causing further delay as the rest of the chimps ran along the river bank, frantically trying to find a way to save their fellow apes. All the while, the apes in the water were screaming so loudly the noise was sure to alert any nearby baboon sentries.

When they were finally able to pull their drowning companions from the river, the eight dozen apes kept moving. The river scare and unintentional noise made them all extremely nervous as they tiptoed, weapons in hand, through the tall grass searching for the baboon's home.

Even though none of the chimps had been in this part of the savannah for years, it was pretty easy to locate the baboon's headquarters for two reasons. One was that snoring monkeys are very loud, and a group of over a hundred sleeping monkeys is deafening. The other reason was that the place the baboons called their "home base" was a massive crater created by a meteor that had imploded in the savannah several million years before. Though so much time had passed, no grass or vegetation had grown in the crater--just rocks and bare dirt stretching for quite a distance.

Fortunately for the apes, there were no baboons keeping guard (probably because the baboons never thought the apes would dare attack them due to their numbers and the river). The crater itself was several hundred feet across, and spread out all over the massive pit were baboons, lots of baboons. Around two hundred monkeys were sprawled out on the rocks and dirt on the crater's floor and all of them were fast asleep, unaware of the upcoming danger.

"Travis," whispered Purcellville, "we need a plan. If we're really going to do this, I say we surround the crater from all sides and..."

Travis interrupted angrily, "I already have a plan, and it's ATTACK!!"

Travis roared like a lion, raised his club high into the air and charged down into the crater. The other chimpanzees followed their leader shouting and roaring and waving their clubs, their spears, and their stones.

Travis rushed to the nearest baboon who had barely awoken; the baboon turned its head looking for the source of the noise and barely had time to scream before Travis slammed his club down on the monkey.

It was full-blown chaos. The chimpanzees made quick work of the nearest baboons, however, the bulk of the baboon force was on the other side of the crater. Some were still stirring while others were already rushing forward to meet their opponents.

Travis in particular was cutting through the baboon lines like they were insects. He was striking any monkey that was in reach of his club, and there were a fair few. Very few of the baboon warriors stood a chance against the massive 200-pound chimpanzee--except one. Travis caught sight of Bruno the baboon king. He, too, was making quick work of any chimpanzees near him. He was in the act of strangling one chimp with his tail and punching the daylights out of another.

When the monkey king caught sight of the ape king he laughed loudly, released the two apes he was fighting, and charged Travis. The chimpanzee showed no sign of fear as the baboon shot toward him. Travis hurled his club at Bruno but the agile monkey dogged the projectile. Travis beat his chest threateningly, and charged. The two titans clashed, rolling around, biting, scratching, and clawing each other.

Up on top of the crater, Purcellville stood alone watching the chaos unfold. He sighed deeply.

"Plush, where are you?" he said sadly to himself. The last thing he expected to hear was a response. From right behind him, he heard a familiar voice say, "Grandpa, we're back."

Purcellville spun around and, to his utter amazement, saw Plush standing behind him. With a rush of emotions, the two apes embraced. Purcellville was the first to speak.

"Plush, you're okay!! You're alive!! I was so worried. AHHH!"

Purcellville suddenly grabbed Plush's arm and pulled Plush behind him, raising his cane defensively; he had caught sight of Peter who had been lingering behind the pair in silence.

"You...YOU'RE THE SNAKE WHO TRIED TO EAT MY GRANDSON," said Purcellville with a mix of fear and anger in his voice.

"Grandpa, wait," said Plush trying to interject, but his voice was drowned out by Peter's.

"SO, YOU'RE THE APE WHO TOOK MY EYE!" said Peter, narrowing his one remaining eye.

Purcellville and Peter stared into each other's eyes (and eye), anger and rage visible in both. Peter seemed ready to spring, but Purcellville stood his ground, cane at the ready.

Plush, fearing a fight was about to break out, leapt in front of the pair, trying to ease the tension.

"Grandpa, stop! This is Peter. He's on our side. He helped me escape from the humans, and he saved my life, and I saved his. We're not enemies," said Plush, hoping this statement would stop the standoff.

Suddenly, a bored voice interrupted the reunion. "Uh, Plush, aren't we supposed to be stopping something important?" said Bongo. He had an odd look on his face like he had forgotten what that important thing was, and the raging battle in front of him was doing nothing to help his memory.

"Right! Peter, listen! We need to stop the fight NOW!" said Plush.

The group rushed down into the crater, but the battle had moved to the opposite side. The fight had reached somewhat of a stalemate;

the remaining chimpanzees had been forced into a cluster and were surrounded on all sides by rows and rows of baboons. It seemed the apes had lost. The only ape who was still fighting was Travis; he was on the far side of the crater, a good distance away from the other chimps.

Travis was on the verge of overpowering Bruno. The two were very closely matched, however, Travis's punches and Travis's blows seemed to do more damage to Bruno than Bruno's strikes did to him.

In a final burst of energy, Bruno managed to kick Travis a full ten feet from his previous position. Bruno was bleeding aggressively, the bones in his tail had been snapped, and it was clear the baboon king was too injured to keep fighting Travis.

Travis could see Bruno getting weaker, and he knew who had to come out on top. The giant chimp charged forward, ready to end the baboon king once and for all when suddenly...

"PROTECT THE KING!" yelled a baboon.

Travis was feet away from Bruno when six large baboons appeared out of nowhere and piled on top of him, biting and scratching. The monkeys were determined not to let Travis get to their king. Until now, all the baboons had been too distracted to help Bruno, but now that the other chimpanzees had been defeated, they were free to fiercely defend their leader.

Travis fought very hard, but every time he struck down one of the baboon warriors, two more appeared, and soon Travis was overpowered. Each of his limbs had been grabbed by a baboon, and together, the monkeys dragged him towards the huddle of trapped apes.

Travis was brought in full view of the rest of his tribe. The monkeys forced him to his knees and turned him to face Bruno. The baboon king picked up Travis's club and was slowly walking towards his opponent. It was clear what was about to happen: the chimpanzees were about to watch a public execution.

Travis struggled so violently, it took half a dozen monkeys to hold him down. Several chimps rushed forward, trying to save their chief, but they were beaten back by the baboon horde.

"THIS IS FOR MY SON!" roared Bruno who was feet away from Travis waving the club, when suddenly a series of loud screams came from the far side of the baboon lines. Everyone turned to see baboons scattering out of the way as Peter the Python cleared a path through the swarm of monkeys, heading right for Travis and Bruno.

(If you didn't know already, monkeys, especially baboons, are generally brave creatures, but they have one common fear: they are terrified of snakes--especially big snakes like Peter. Peter's particular species, the African rock python, has a reputation for being able to kill and eat even the strongest monkeys with ease. When Peter showed himself to the baboons, they were instinctively horrified, and parted ways for the great snake in droves.)

Then, from behind Peter, Bongo ran forward into full view of everyone. Bongo caught sight of Bruno and ran forward, shouting, "HI, DAD." When he reached Bruno, he threw his arms out and hugged the larger baboon.

Bruno stood rooted to the spot. He stared down at Bongo with astonishment and confusion. "Bongo...but...but I thought...you're alive...but the apes...?"

"Dad, the apes had nothing to do with it. I was kidnapped by humans," said Bongo, still hugging his dad.

There was a moment of silence broken only when Travis shouted. "I TOLD YOU WE DIDN'T KIDNAP YOUR SON, BUT YOU STUPID MONKEYS WOULDN'T BELIEVE US."

"SHUT UP!" yelled several baboons who were trying to listen; even the trapped chimpanzees were straining to hear Bongo and Bruno's conversation.

When Plush came forward, there was quite an uproar, and Bongo had to stop the baboons from dog-piling on him.

"PLUSH...BUT YOU'RE SUPPOSED TO BE DEAD," shouted Travis as he saw Plush. Bongo had to explain that Plush had also been kidnapped and that he had helped him and Peter escape from the humans.

All the apes and all the baboons were overwhelmed with curiosity, and the clubbing to death was suspended for the time being. It was clear that they wanted to know everything that had happened.

(Remember this was the first time any animal had ever returned alive after being taken by humans, so naturally everyone was curious.)

Plush was aware of hundreds of eyes on him. Peter had slumped over and was slowly inching away from the group and towards the edge of the crater. Bongo had nervously slid out of view leaving Plush in the spotlight.

"Well, it's a long story," said Plush. He had never stood before a crowd like this, and he struggled trying to find the courage to speak. Then, he caught sight of his grandfather Purcellville smiling encouragingly at him from the back of the baboon crowd. The monkeys were too busy watching Plush to notice the old ape standing among them. Plush took a deep breath and began to explain. He told everyone about how Bongo had been kidnapped several days before he had. He explained how he had tried to sneak into the cow field, how he stepped into the trap, and how the humans had captured him.

Plush talked and talked, and Bongo spoke up several times, adding the details about fruit fights and single-handedly subduing the car-creature, though he spent most of the time absentmindedly wrestling his tail. Plush decided to not mention the fact he had been able to learn and speak the human language, and, thankfully, Bongo had either forgotten or didn't think it was worth mentioning. When Plush got to the part about the ape corpses hanging from the ceiling of the warehouse, even Travis looked shocked.

All the animals were fascinated by his description of the human city, the tall buildings stretching miles into the sky, and the hundreds of car creatures zooming by at impossible speeds.

When Plush spoke about Percy's death, many of the baboons looked sadly at the ground, and Bongo began to sob so aggressively he started choking. Plush also left out the part where he had let the humans live, making it seem like he had beaten them, and they had simply run away, which was close enough to the truth. When he finished speaking, there was a deathly silence as the apes and monkeys tried to comprehend the full story.

Eventually, Bongo broke the silence.

"So, uh, what happens now?"

Not one of the monkeys or apes had an answer.

SEAN PATRICK JOYCE

CHAPTER 28
The Only Witness

The rest of the night was a daze for Plush. The apes sent messenger birds out to the northern apes informing them of the situation, and then the negotiations began. Purcellville did most of the talking as Travis and Bruno were unable to face each other without throwing hands. Purcellville was very clear with the baboons when explaining the food shortages of the apes---the apes were in desperate need of food. Bruno, however, made it clear that if he were to share the baboons' plentiful supply of food, the apes had to give the baboons something in return. When Purcellville asked what Bruno would want from the apes, the monkey king had no response, unable to think of anything until Plush stepped forward and offered a suggestion.

"We can teach you how to make tools and weapons. Only the apes have that knowledge, but we would be willing to share it in exchange for regular supplies of food--at least until the famine ends."

This proposal was met with cheers and joy from the baboons, and it was agreed that the following morning Purcellville and several other apes would meet the baboons at the river and would begin to teach their craftsmanship skills in exchange for nuts, fruits, meats and berries.

Finally, after years and years of conflict and years and years of raiding, plundering, and harming each other, the two species were finally at peace. The issue had been solved by four animals who were thrown together by chance, but who stayed together by choice, united by a common purpose.

Although there were many injuries, not a single ape or monkey died in the conflict. The only casualty had been poor Percy the parrot.

As the apes began to depart back to their forest, Plush caught sight of Peter slithering off in the opposite direction of the ape forest. Determined to speak to him before he left, Plush hurried after Peter and caught up fairly quickly.

"Peter! HEY, PETER!" The snake stopped and turned.

"What is it, Ape?" said Peter, shaking his head in exhaustion.

"It's...just I..." Plush had no idea what to say. His brain was overwhelmed and tired, but finally he found the strength to say,

"Thank you...for everything. I owe you my life."

Peter gave him a small smile. "I appreciate that, Ape, but really it's me who should be thanking you. You defeated the humans, you inspired us to escape, and you saved both your tribe and Bongo's. None of that would have been possible without you."

"No," said Plush. "You were the one who knew how to escape. It was your plan. You saved me from the waterfall, and fought the humans, and I would have never been able to stop the tribes fighting if you hadn't helped."

Peter pondered Plush's words for a moment.

"I guess that means we're even," said Peter.

"I guess so," said Plush.

"Listen, Ape, I won't mention your whole speaking human thing. I hope you find how you can do that," said Peter.

"I hope so, too," said Plush. "So what are you gonna do now, Peter?"

The python did the closest thing to shrugging a snake could do. "I guess the one thing I was meant to do: go back to being a lone predator. I will stay away from the apes and baboons, find some nice cave in the hills, and settle down."

Peter turned and continued to slither away.

"Wait! One last thing," said Plush in a slight panic.

Peter turned, "What is it, Ape?" he said.

"Well...will I ever see you again?" asked Plush.

Peter paused and then sadly shook his head. "I don't think so. Our teamwork was necessary to escape and survive. We have done both those things. You don't need an old snake complicating your life...goodbye, Plush." Peter turned and slithered away into the night.

"Goodbye, Peter," said Plush quietly. He stood for a while watching the tall savannah grass swaying in the wind. Then he turned and walked back the opposite way.

As Plush made his way back to his forest, a strange sensation gripped him. Even though he and Peter had said their farewells, Plush had a funny feeling his adventures with Peter the Python were far from over.

With a sense of completion, Plush reached the river and carefully crossed it, clambering over the tree. It wasn't until he reached the other side that he realized which tree it was.

"My...MY...HOUSE!" roared Plush in a mix of surprise, anger, and utter confusion as he turned to a pair of nearby chimps who had just finished crossing the log.

"MY HOUSE! WHAT HAPPENED TO MY...WHY IS MY HOUSE ...?" Plush was babbling, filled with outrage.

"PLUSH, it's not worth screaming over," said Purcellville.

"Apenstein said we can stay with him until we find a new tree."

"But, Grandpa, the tree, what why...?"

"Not now! There is something far more important we need to discuss." Purcellville set off walking towards the ape forest. Plush followed, not sure what his grandfather would say.

They made their way to Apenstein's tree and clambered onto one of the large low hanging branches.

"Plush, I need to know exactly what happened to the humans," said Purcellville.

"What, why?" said Plush, confused. "They're dead. They have to be!"

"You can't know that for sure," said Purcellville. "You said they were able to get to their feet and run away. We need to know if they still pose a threat to our tribe."

"One had a broken arm and an arrow stabbed into its leg and the other had its waist bitten into by Peter, and they were already hurt from their car creature crashing. You weren't there, Grandpa. I saw how hurt they were; they were starving and sick. They would surely have bled to death or died of starvation."

Purcellville turned to Apenstein. "What do you think, Albert? You're the Healer."

232

"Well," said Apenstein, "I'm no expert on humans, but I'm with Plush on this one. It's highly unlikely they lasted this long, and even if they did survive, chances are, they're not coming back here anytime soon."

Despite being relieved by Albert's expert opinion, Plush couldn't keep it a secret any longer. He had to tell somebody soon, even if it made him look crazy. He felt he would explode from the pressure of keeping something like this a secret if he didn't tell his grandfather.

"Grandpa, there's something I need to tell you," said Plush, not sure how to reveal something so absurd and unexplainable. He opened his mouth and started from the beginning. He explained how he had been listening to the humans for days and days and how slowly their unknown chatter became more and more audible and understandable. He explained how he had spoken to the crowd of humans and all he had been able to decipher from overhearing the humans speak. He explained how hearing him speak had been what made the humans flee in terror. Surprisingly, Purcellville and Apenstein were not as surprised as he thought they should be. They listened and shared knowing glances but neither spoke until Plush had finished explaining. There was a long pause before his grandfather spoke.

"Plush, you're not crazy, and you certainly don't have magic powers or some other nonsense."

"Then how could I understand them? It's not right. No chimpanzee can speak or understand human language. It's not possible!"

Purcellville looked at the ground. He took a deep breath and spoke, "Plush...have you ever noticed the...differences between the three of us and the rest of the tribe? The fact we all look slightly different from the other apes or how only the three of us have white spots on our foreheads?"

Plush shrugged, "They're family traits and birthmarks. We're not from this forest, so it makes sense we would be a little different. Why...?"

"Plush, listen. Apenstein and I have suspected this for years, but your abilities confirm it...Plush, when Apenstein and I first arrived here, this forest was nothing like it is now. The chimpanzees here were basic and animalistic; they didn't even have an advanced language like we do now--just some hunting calls. Our old forest was far more advanced than this one was when we arrived. We had far greater tools, a more complex language, and leadership system. Apenstein and I have integrated those systems into this forest over the years."

"I'm confused," said Plush. "Are you saying the three of us are..."

"Not chimpanzees," said Purcellville, finishing the sentence for him. Plush felt overwhelmed with this unexpected information, but the more he thought about, the more it made sense. Maybe the fact he had been small, skinny, and weird-looking wasn't because he was deformed or a runt! And why had his grandfather always seemed so much smarter than the other apes? It was impossible, crazy, insane...but it made sense.

"Why, why did you never tell me this?" said Plush, rolling this impossible realization through his mind.

"Plush, I promised your parents I would protect you even if that meant keeping secrets. I'm sorry I never told you this before, but you were young and reckless. I wanted to keep my theories a secret from the rest of the tribe."

"Why?"

"Plush, you know what these apes are like. If they found out we were something different, they would probably kick us out. I also believe the reason the humans attacked our forest was because they knew or suspected we were different somehow. They killed almost all of our family. They probably thought they wiped us out and, thanks to you, our secret remains safe. Bongo has probably forgotten the fact you could speak, and it seems the large crowd you spoke to believed your presence was some sort of trick. The two humans who captured you are most likely dead by now, and even if they do survive, I doubt other humans will take the word of two people who were lost in the wilderness for days and days very seriously. Plush, it seems the humans are no longer a threat to us."

There was a moment where Plush actually believed this statement, a moment where he felt safe and content. But that feeling was shattered by a sudden memory. He remembered being tied down on an operating table by the human. He remembered when he had begged Dr. Nile for : "Food."

"Plush! This is no time to be thinking about FOOD," said Purcellville. Plush was shaking. His hands were a blur as he looked up at his grandfather, dread and panic radiating from him.

"Plush, what's wrong?" said Purcellville.

Plush did not respond, fear and terror making it impossible for him to speak.. It didn't matter if Big Ben and Little John survived or not. It didn't matter if the crowd believed he was really a talking ape or not. Someone else had witnessed him speak.

Plush somehow found the words to say, "Grandpa, I'm so sorry, but you're wrong. Someone does know about us. A human...a very dangerous human..."

EPILOGUE

A small group of children from Ng'ombe Mji were walking back to their village, carrying the heavy buckets of water they had collected from a nearby river (the same river that separated chimpanzee and baboon territory). The sun had risen fairly high that morning. The path was not really a path; they would just follow the footsteps from the previous day, winding through the tall grass that, at times, reached over six feet tall. The villagers knew the tall dense grass very well, and they knew the dangers of the local wildlife, so the group was constantly monitoring their surroundings, though they did not expect any aggression from the wildlife as their village had been part of this savannah for so long; the wildlife had adjusted to the humans living here and rarely showed aggression towards them. In fact, the wild creatures rarely showed themselves. All the animals feared humans-- even the strongest lions or the most daring hyenas kept their distance, and the humans knew this. As a result, the adults would often entrust the youngest members of the village with these mundane tasks, obviously under the impression that as long as the kids stayed in a group, they were relatively safe.

So when a strange moaning noise came from a nearby cluster of particularly dense grass, the children were quite alarmed. They stopped in their tracks, looking around for the origin of the strange noise. Had the sound been any different, the villagers would have simply quickened their pace, but this sound made them stop. The grass was too tall and dense to see what was making the noise, but this sound made them pause. This noise sounded distinctly familiar. However, they were all terrified of wavering off the path.

Eventually, one of the kids--the oldest boy in the group-- stepped forward daringly, not wanting to look cowardly in front of his companions (several of whom were girls). He slowly picked up a large stone and began creeping toward the source of the noise. Behind him,

237

the rest of the group began to follow. The grass eventually gave way, and the kid leading the group screamed.

Laying in the grass, his face swollen and bloody and his jaw was broken at an unnatural angle, was Big Ben. Ben's eyes were closed, his skin was red and sunburned, and his clothes were ragged and covered in blood.

The group of kids gathered around the body, scared but curious. The older boy however took charge immediately.

"You two," he pointed at the two youngest kids in the group. "Run back to the village. Tell them there is a man out here who needs help." The two youngest kids ran off, the remaining kids gathered around Big Ben, their minds filled with both horror and curiosity.

"Is… is…is he…dead?" said one of the kids, trembling with fear.

"No, he's breathing," said another kid.

Suddenly, the entire group jumped at the sound of a soft voice, a dry gagging voice as if the person who spoke had the worst sore throat on earth.

"Help…" said the voice, but it was not coming from Big Ben but from several dozen feet behind the big man. Moreover, the voice was speaking English, not the native Swahili. The kids moved forward through the dense, tall grass and saw Little John lying upright against a rock; his left leg and right arm were both bent at grotesque angles, obviously broken. Little John was shaking, his face trembling.

The kids immediately offered him some water, which he silently accepted, gulping down the liquid with his uninjured arm.

"What on earth happened to you two?" said the older boy, no longer in Swahili but in English, realizing this man was not native to the area. It took Little John a while to respond. His mouth was trembling so violently it seemed he was unable to articulate any words clearly. Through his blabbering, the village children could make out only some of what he was saying.

"I…w…we…escaped…terrible."

"What, what did you escape?" said one of the kids, looking at his friends with confusion and noticeable fear.

Little John mumbled several more inaudible phrases. Finally, however, he found the strength to whisper, "It.. it…was…a m…monster, noo… a…a DEMON."

MEET THE AUTHOR

Sean P. Joyce isn't your typical 15-year-old. While most kids his age are stuck on level 30 of some video game, Sean is busy creating a whole world of ape warriors, jungle raids, and fierce fights for survival.

The adventures of Plush, his fearless and often misunderstood ape, began as bedtime tales and grew into full-blown epics through his imagination. With the help of an English teacher and a school writing class, Sean took his storytelling to the next level and wrote his debut novel, *The Great Esc-APE*.

Sean P. Joyce is a 15-year-old storyteller with a bold imagination. From a young age, Sean was known for spinning tales, often centered on a mischievous and brave chimp named Plush. These stories began as animated conversations at home, evolving over time into a full-blown universe brimming with humor, heart, and high-stakes action.

His journey from spoken word to written page took off when his exceptional English teacher introduced a creative writing course. What started as a school project quickly became something more: a chance to share the world he'd been building for years. That's when *The Great Esc-APE* was born.

THE END